MW00912340

ROAD WITHOUT END

BY RON KEARSE

Copyright © 2013 by Ron Kearse
First Edition – March 2013

ISBN
978-1-77097-562-0 (Hardcover)
978-1-77097-563-7 (Paperback)
978-1-77097-564-4 (eBook)

All rights reserved.

No part of this publication may be reproduced in any form, or by any means, electronic or mechanical, including photocopying, recording, or any information browsing, storage, or retrieval system, without permission in writing from the publisher.

Published by:

FriesenPress
Suite 300 – 852 Fort Street
Victoria, BC, Canada V8W 1H8

www.friesenpress.com

Distributed to the trade by The Ingram Book Company

May 23, 2014

Shannon;
Thank you and please
enjoy!
Cheers;
Ron Kearse

PART ONE

There's nothing like a good cup of coffee and a fantastic song to get you started in the morning. The stereo's blasting *Sultans of Swing* by Dire Straits, and I tap out time on the steering wheel. The sun is shining; the snow has almost melted, and I'm looking forward to a great summer. This feels like I'm travelling down a road to adventure, even though I'm only going to work.

I live in a village called Angus, just outside of Camp Borden, a military base about an hour's drive north of Toronto. I work on the Base and make this trip every day. Dad used to be in the military, but he retired five years ago. He and mom have always liked this area, so when they saw an opportunity, they bought a house here and stayed. I'm still living at home with them and my two brothers, Frank and Pete.

I drive where nothing but thick, dark green forest shields my peripheral vision, like a long green wall on either side of the road. Those walls stretch ahead of me, hiding every curve with yet more green. They seem to guide my way along the strip of pavement until I reach the main gate of the military base.

The road widens, and a small, nondescript guardhouse sits stoically in the middle of it. Barricades stretch across the asphalt from either side of this building. It's as though you're about to cross the border into some other country.

I see two shadows moving about through the windows of the guardhouse. One of the shadows opens a door to the side of the building and steps into the March sun. He's an older man with a white handlebar moustache; he's wearing a Commissionaire's uniform. He's been doing this job for fifteen years, and every morning when he comes out of the building we go through the same ritual.

He glances at my pass to the Base stuck to the windshield, then he looks into the driver's window at me and smiles.

"Good mornin' Neil," he says.

"Hey Len! How 're ya doin'?"

"Never in my life have I had a better day!"

I like hearing him say that. It's Len's standard answer every morning. So I ask him that question every day just to hear him say it. Len walks over, lifts the barricade that spans the blacktop and waves me through.

Winding through the streets of Base Borden, I glance at the houses, and each looks exactly the same as the next. Every address on every street looks just the same as the address beside it or across the road. There's nothing on the outside of any of the houses that make them stand out. No gardens in the yards, no additions to the individual buildings, none of the unique things that you see in other communities. These places are cheaply built, functional, and temporary. It's scarier than suburbia. I drive on.

I whistle along to the radio as I pull into the fenced-in lot that spans the front of the building where I report for work. I've been working here, temporarily, for two years now, just like the rest of my ground crew. That means that every six months the suits lay us off then renew our contracts so we can work another six months. I don't know why it's done that way. It's a government decision, go figure! I park the car, and it looks to me like all the guys are here with their morning coffees in hand. There's Johnny, the brunt of all the practical jokes the guys can think of.

Johnny is a bit slow—some would call him simple. He wouldn't say shit if he was eating it and is forever spilling his coffee all over himself in his nervousness. I remember the time some of the office staff found Johnny in one of the lockers after the grounds crews had left for their work sites. Nobody could figure out where that banging was coming from, until they followed the sound. It was Art and Nick that had stuffed him in there, poor guy. And did those two ever catch supreme hell from the big boss when they got back that afternoon.

From inside the car, I can't hear what's being said yet, but Johnny's waving his hands in the air as he seems to be making a point to Art and Nick.

Art and Nick, now there's a real pair of characters. They call themselves *The Dynamic Duo*, everyone else calls them *Assholes*. They're like two bad little boys. They're always joking, roughhousing, or pulling stupid pranks. Like the time that they put salt into the sugar jar at work, and then laughed their fool heads off when they watched our faces as we took our first sips of coffee that morning. That's Art and Nick. Their long-suffering wives must have grey hair because of their antics away from work. I can only imagine the things they get up to, and somehow I don't think I want to know.

The two of them are close friends who sometimes hate each other's guts. Nick does this work as much as he can. Art, in the meantime, raises horses in the summer and does this every spring and winter to cover a lot of his farming costs. He sometimes hires Johnny when they take the horses to shows and rodeos across the country.

There's Wilf, the old Saskatchewan farm boy. He's the father figure of the group. In fact, he reminds me a lot of my grandad. Sometimes you can almost feel the strength and wisdom behind Wilf's faded, blue eyes while he's talking to you. That's the same feeling I used to get around my grandad.

Wilf's going to retire soon, and I don't know what he's going to do then because he lives for this job. He says he's got some projects going when he does retire, but they won't last forever. He sometimes talks about taking his wife out to Vancouver Island, and maybe buying some property around Comox. They were there some years ago, and they fell in love with the place. They are hoping to go back some day.

I park the car, turn off the engine, and get out to join the rest of the crew. We say our good mornings and hang around sipping our morning coffees for a bit. Then with rakes, shovels, and push brooms in hand, we get into the back of a half-ton truck and are on our way to be dropped off at our various work sites for the day.

Along the way to our work areas, the truck slows down and pulls over to the side of the road. The three of us in the back of the truck look at each other, and we all have smirks on our faces.

We're stopped beside a small clearing in the woods, and the only thing present is a dark blue, portable toilet.

"Here we go again," says Nick, rolling his eyes.

The door of the truck cab bursts open and Art bounds out quickly heading for the Johnny-on-the-Spot. He goes in and shuts the door.

We all smile and shake our heads because Art does this about three times a week. We usually don't mind because this holds us up for about twenty minutes, and who in their right mind is in a hurry to get to work?

Nick's drumming his fingers impatiently on the side of the truck, and finally says, "That does it." He vaults over the side of the truck, runs up to the door of the john, and opens it wide. He leans beside the open door smiling at us and pointing at Art. We burst into laughter, especially Johnny who holds his hand over his mouth trying to keep from cackling.

There Art sits with his pants around his ankles, and a cigarette dangling from the left corner of his mouth. Without blinking an eye Art smiles at us and waves. Then he unrolls some toilet paper and waves it like a streamer around his head. We break into whoops and applause as Nick slams the door on Art and comes back to our truck.

Art emerges from the john a few moments later, shaking his head and laughing. He walks to the cab of the truck, points at Nick, and says, "I'm gonna get you." Then he laughs again as he gets into the cab and shuts the door.

Nick looks at me, smiles, and says, "He *will* get me for this, the bastard." He shakes his head, then says, "By the way, you and I are workin' together today."

That's great news because I like working with Nick. He cracks me up. His imitations of Monty Python characters are great. I usually try to join in the fun by trying to speak the same way, but I always fuck it up. My voice will crack, or I laugh so hard that I can't say anything.

In a short few minutes, the truck stops on the shoulder of the road and Nick and I jump off the back and collect our equipment for the day's work ahead. The day goes by as usual, Nick with his never-ending wise cracks and Monty Python imitations, and me trying to work but laughing so hard I can barely concentrate on what I'm doing. And all too soon, when Nick and I work together, the workday starts to wind down.

We collect our tools and wait for that familiar khaki-coloured half-ton to take us back to the work yard. Today happens to be payday, so when we're finally back there, it's time to collect our cheques. I open the envelope, and my heart feels like its fallen and collided with the soles of my feet. My mouth is hanging open in disbelief, and I feel like I've been kicked in the gut. It's a fuckin' pink slip.

I feel a knot in my gut as I consider a possibility, *What if they've found out I'm gay, and they're letting me go because of it? No, don't be an asshole, Neil.* I answer myself, *It's not that way at all.* But this is really strange because we usually don't get temporary lay off slips until later in the season. I walk over to see what's happening with the other guys.

All of the crew congregates in the parking lot as we usually do at this time of the week. I notice the other guys all have bewildered looks on their faces. Art's head is shaking as he approaches us, and at the same time, he's scratching his head in disbelief. "I've got bad news guys, this time the lay-off is permanent. I guess that we should have seen this coming," he says as we gather. "The boss says the government is cutting back, and we're one of the first to go."

Johnny pipes up, "But they kept renewing our contracts, so I thought that things would be different this time. I thought they'd take us on permanent soon. They would've, wouldn't they Art?"

"Johnny," says Nick curtly, "The pink slip means we're gone." Johnny looks at the pink slip once more, and his eyes slowly turn to the ground with a look of sad acceptance.

Nick breathes a heavy sigh and strokes his blond beard. He stares blankly at the ground. I've never seen him so seriously deep in thought. I can hardly hear him as he speaks.

"I promised the family a camping trip to Algonquin Park this year. How am I going tell them it isn't happening?" He sighs.

Wilf nods his head, but there's a strange look in his eyes. I've seen him wear it before. It's the look he gets when he's confirmed a suspicion, or has come to a conclusion. Then Wilf chuckles and begins to speak.

"Gentlemen," says Wilf, "for a while now, some of my friends have said to me things like, 'Wilf, don't you think that it's time you retired? Wilf, don't you think you're a little too old to be doing this type of work? Wilf, maybe you and the good-wife should buy an Airstream and go travellin' for a while.'"

Wilf looks at us and a broad smile slowly draws across his mouth. Then he says, "I'll tell you what I'm thinkin'. The good-wife and me have been talkin' for some time now about just packin' everything and moving to Vancouver Island."

We're silent as we listen to him.

"Guys," he says, "this little pink slip just tells me that now's the time to do it. I will never have to get up for work again. Maybe it's a good time for all of us to make the changes we want to make."

He shakes our hands as he addresses us.

"Art. Nick. Neil. Johnny," says Wilf, "it's been great working with you all, but I have to go home. I've got a new life to prepare myself for. Aggie's gonna love this."

With that, he kisses the pink slip, and he leaves the small circle of men and walks to his car.

"Wilf," calls Art, "keep in touch!"

Wilf stops, turns back to us and announces, "We're going to move to Comox. I'll let you guys know when our farewell party is."

Wilf heads over to his car and unlocks the door of his '65 Parisienne, gets inside, and starts the ignition. We stand quietly and watch as he backs his car out of its parking space. I can see him waving and smiling at us as he drives the car out the front gate of the yard, leaving the spring dust swirling in its tailwind.

We all look at each other and smile sadly.

"Well," says Art, "he seems to be happy."

"And here I was worried about him," I say.

"I don't know about you guys," Art continues, "but I'm gonna get drunk. Anybody wanna grab some beer with me and come back to my place?"

Nick and Johnny are up for it. I don't feel like drinking. I just wanna be alone. So I say my good-byes to them.

"It's been good workin' with you guys," I say, shaking Art's hand.

"Hey, we'll see you at Wilf's farewell party, whenever that'll be," says Art.

I shake hands with Johnny and Nick. They head over to Art's place for some serious drinkin', and I want some time to think about what's just happened. Who knows, maybe Wilf's right? This might be the chance for me to move to Toronto like I've always wanted to.

I walk to my dad's car. I take one last look around the gravel-covered yard while I lean on the open driver's door. My eyes scan back and forth over the yard's entirety. I get into the car and leave.

∞

This has happened so damned fast that I still don't believe it's happening at all. And yet, listening to Wilf's decision, I feel like there's been some finality put in place.

My mind is so preoccupied. I remember almost nothing about the drive home. The car comes to a halt in my parents' driveway. I turn the engine off and leave the radio on.

"*This is radio news at the top of the hour,*" interrupts an announcer authoritatively. "*More news coming out of Harrisburg Pennsylvania where a meltdown occurred at a nuclear power plant on Wednesday morning. Reactor number two at Metropolitan Edison's Three Mile Island power plant was—*" CLICK!

I angrily turn the damn radio off. I'm not in the mood for anymore bad news, and today there's nothing but bullshit everywhere. I sit quietly in the car spacing out, my mind wandering, my thoughts scattering. My fingers slowly stroke the right side of my moustache as I sit motionless and stare ahead of me. I miss the guys already. I'm thinking of what Wilf said to us, *"Maybe it's a good time for all of us to make the changes we want to make."*

That's not a bad idea. I could really get into living in Toronto. Ah shit. The neighbour in the house two doors down is playing that goddamned disco tape of his, again.

Unfortunately anytime I'm in Toronto, disco is all I hear at the gay hangouts. It's all the same with that stupid thump, thump, thump of a beat, and brainless lyrics. But as I sit here, it's those brainless lyrics that keep echoing in my head as Blondie's *Heart of Glass* is being blasted from my neighbour's speakers.

As much as I hate to admit it, I'm starting to like that song. It makes me think of Jeff.

I met him the last time I was in Toronto. What a guy. We met on a Friday night at a club called The Manatee. He was standing by the dance floor, just taking in the entire scene. He was tall and thin, with an army style haircut and moustache. He wore a plaid shirt, a pair of 501 jeans, and a pair of black motorcycle boots. He didn't own a motorcycle, but that didn't seem to matter.

We had a couple of beer together, smoked a joint, then went back to the bus terminal to get my bag, which I had stashed in a locker. I remember it seemed like Blondie's song was all we heard while we were walking along Yonge Street to his apartment.

We hit the sack as soon as we got to his place. Sex with Jeff was terrific. I remember he wore his boots the whole time, and wanted me to wear my denim jacket and a cowboy hat he had on hand while we were fucking. At one point on the Saturday, Jeff got me to lay on his couch while I was buck-ass naked. He said that he thought that men with cigars were sexy, so he lit a cigar and handed to me. I laid there with this cigar in my mouth while that dirty bastard snapped Polaroids of me with a hard-on. That's okay, I didn't mind a bit. He gave me a couple of the photos, and I can tell you those are two photos that I keep well hidden.

I can't remember how many times we screwed around that weekend, but we finally got out of bed on Sunday at noon. I'd never had sex like that before, but I sure as hell would like to again. We've talked a couple of times on the phone since then, and I'd like to spend another weekend with him soon.

I smile as I think about Jeff, lean forward, and rest my chin on the steering wheel. My chest presses against the car horn, and I'm slapped back to Earth.

That's when I look toward the house and see my father looking through the living room window to see what's going on. He looks concerned and motions to me to get out of the car. I shake my head to quit daydreaming, and any excitement I was feeling is instantly gone.

Dad's walking toward me with a big smile on his face.

"That's not usual for you to be sitting quietly like that in the car. Usually you've got that disco blastin'—"

"Dad, I hate disco, I like rock."

"Well whatever it's called, you've usually got it blastin'."

He sees that I'm not responding to his kidding like I usually do, "What's up son? What's the matter?"

"I got laid off today, Dad, and it's permanent this time."

"C'mon," he says, "let's go inside and talk about it."

He puts his hand on my shoulder and leads me into the house. After taking off our shoes at the door, we enter the living room where I flop like a dead weight onto the couch. It wouldn't be so bad if the layoff wasn't permanent this time.

Frank is sprawled in an overstuffed, rust-coloured, swivel chair across from me. He barely acknowledges my presence as I sit down. He has one foot on the floor and the other leg lazily resting over the arm of the chair. His face is buried in today's edition of the Toronto Star. I can hear the muffled sounds of a Kiss album coming from behind the closed door of Pete's room down the hall.

"Hey Frank, how's it goin'?" I smile trying to start a conversation.

"Not bad," he responds, his face still buried in his paper.

"I'll get us a beer," Dad says as he disappears into the kitchen.

"Was that Neil that I heard come in?" I can hear my mother ask.

"Yeah," Dad answers as I hear the fridge door open, followed by the sound of two bottles clinking together.

"We're just gonna have a little talk. He got permanently laid off today."

"What!" exclaims mom. "What's he gonna do now?"

"Mother, he'll be fine. He just needs to sort some things out."

"Well, there aren't any jobs around here to speak of—"

"Jesus woman, there you go again. Will you listen to yourself?"

Frank glances at me from behind the paper, as the sound of our parents voices intermingle in the kitchen.

We both smile, shake our heads, and roll our eyes. Here they go again.

"Sometimes I think they like needlin' each other," says Frank.

I agree with a chuckle.

"So you got the boot permanently?"

"Yeah."

"Ah shit man, are you alright?"

"I'll be okay, thanks."

"Well, if you and dad have to talk, I'll go into the kitchen and help Mom."

"Sure."

Dad comes back into the living room and hands me a bottle of beer, while Frank goes into the kitchen with Mom.

"Thanks Dad," I say as he sits beside me. He puts his arm around my shoulder and says, "So talk to me."

"Well, Mom's right. What am I gonna do? There is only seasonal work around here at best."

Dad gets up and walks to the living room window, one hand holding his beer and the other in his pants pocket. He fixes his gaze out the window at the quiet village street that we live on, "I'm afraid there's no easy answers in this kind of a situation, Son."

"I guess I'm thinkin' that maybe it's about time that I move to Toronto."

Dad silently continues to stare out the window. I can hear the murmur of Mom and Frank talking in the kitchen.

"Dad, did you hear me?"

"Well," he says, "you've talked about it a lot lately, and you sure go down there quite a bit. You seem to have met a few people that you could probably stay with for a few days while you're looking for work. Who was that fella you mentioned the last time you were down there? What's his name, Jeff? You get along well with him don't ya?"

My eyebrows raise as I say, "Yeah Dad, we get along *really* well."

"Well, there you go," he says. "Give him a call next week. See if he can put you up for a couple of days. I'm sure that he wouldn't mind"

I know that he wouldn't mind, I think.

"I guess you've already worked out a plan of action. I always said you were a smart kid," my father says as he smiles at me.

We talk for a little while longer, and I tell Dad about how I'm going to miss the guys. He seems to take a special interest when I tell him how some of Wilf's parting words stand out in my mind.

"I think that you should go out with your buddies tonight and celebrate," Dad says excitedly.

"Celebrate what?"

"Your new freedom. Wilf's absolutely right, this is a chance for you to make some changes in your life. Changes that *you* want to make. Didn't you tell me just last week that there's an audition at your drama group tonight?"

"Yeah, so?"

"I think you should go."

"I'm not sure that I want to audition for a play right now."

"You don't have to audition, you just have to be there."

"I don't feel like goin' out, Dad. That's why I didn't go over to Art's after work with the other guys."

"Neil, it looks to me like you're already making plans to do some things that you want to do anyway."

I pause, for it occurs to me that Dad's right. Suddenly the idea of being with the folks at the theatre group is very appealing.

"You can take the next week to figure out what you're going to do. But I think that you already know what you're going to be doing," Dad says, with a smile.

I'm silent. *It would be nice to be at the audition tonight,* I think, *then go for a few beer and some laughs later. Maybe I could get into that.* I nod in agreement with Dad.

"Go wash your hands, you guys," calls Mom from the kitchen, "dinner's ready."

∞

I'm sitting in the theatre, and I'm listening to the excited chatter of the people around me. I got a ride from Jim, the soundman for the theatre group who lives a couple of blocks from me.

He's in the theatre's control booth at the back of the auditorium, getting the sound ready for tonight. He's got music on the turntable as he always does. He hires himself out as a weekend DJ, and he sure has the equipment and the set-up to do it successfully. Two turntables, microphones, speakers, lights, a couple of sound mixers, and a collection of twelve inch singles that would make Studio 54 burn with envy. Maybe that's an exaggeration, but you get my drift.

He loads everything up in his panel truck and drives to the many gigs that he has from Barrie to Collingwood. He never goes far, but these gigs keep him busy. Right now he's assaulting my ears with one of the seemingly endless extended versions of Y.M.C.A. by the Village People. I catch him as he's walking down the aisle from the booth to the stage.

"Hey Jim!"

"That's me!"

"You don't have any Patti Smith or Iggy Pop in that record collection of yours do you?"

"No."

"Anything by The Clash or Elvis Costello?"

"No way!"

"Okay, forget I asked."

It's hard to say just how many people are here tonight, maybe twenty or thirty. I don't recognize a lot of them. Small groups of three to five people are spread throughout the seating space. The loudest noise is coming from Dave, Phil, and Ian. The three of them are among the craziest bastards I've ever known.

Dave is the most reserved of the three. He's the type of guy that every woman likes to mother because he's so cute and sweet. But don't let his quiet exterior fool you, he's the instigator of the trio. He'll suggest things to the other two, who'll carry the deeds to conclusion and get into trouble, and all the while, Dave stands by looking innocent.

Phil is the lanky Englishman who—like Nick—seems to know every Monty Python skit ever written. He's dashing, handsome, charming, and well dressed. He's started a bit of a trend around the base by wearing a pair of tan-coloured Frye boots with his pant legs tucked inside of them. Now it seems that a lot of other guys have taken to wearing Frye boots exactly the same way.

Ian is our Tarzan-the-Ape-Man, swinging from the chandeliers and then landing in the punch bowl at every party. He's a jock, and there's not a sports team on the base that he doesn't play on. He's landed in the drunk tank a couple of times, just for getting rowdy. He can be embarrassing to be around sometimes. Especially during episodes when he gets slobbering drunk and he loudly drools, "Geesh I love you guysh! Geesh, I love you guysh!" That's when we usually take what's left of him back to the barracks and put him to bed.

I'm surprised they're not up dancing to the music like they usually would be by now. These guys don't just dance, they make a total production of it. They remind me of three roosters the way they swagger, pivot, jump and spin in unison. To watch them reminds me of a series of basketball moves set to music. They've won several local dance contests because of their unique performance, and all of this seems to attract the women, which is exactly the reason they do it. Anyway, things are going to get started in about five minutes, so there's an excited yet nervous buzz in the air as there always is just before an audition.

This is our second theatrical production in the new theatre that the good Prime Minister in Ottawa built for the base this year, and it's really impressive. It's in the Buell Building, which is the Base Borden recreation centre. It's in the same complex as the local public swimming pool, gym, and a restaurant/cafeteria. Everything worked excellently during our last production, so we're looking forward to this one. This theatre may be small, but it's modern and quite cozy, just an excellent way for a live theatre space to be. Thank you, Prime Minister Trudeau!

I open the small mustard-coloured book that each of us was given upon entering. It's the script of the play that we'll be performing, which is called *Leaving Home* by David French. It's supposed to be quite dramatic. I'm just looking over the cast of characters in the play, when I hear a voice call me,

"Neil! I'm glad you're here!"

I glance up from the script to see Cheryl approaching me. Cheryl is president of the theatre group. She's a big woman, who commands attention wherever she goes, if only for her brilliant colours. She's always wearing large, brightly coloured hats and brilliant muumuus, with matching shoes, sunglasses and handbags. Her husband is an officer in camp, and he's being posted to Base Suffield outside of Medicine Hat, Alberta this summer. I'm gonna miss Cheryl because, when we're together, we have a blast! In fact, she's one of the few people who I've told I'm gay. When we're together we'll always rate the guys around us: he's cute, what do you think? A nine? or, he's got a nice ass! Definitely a ten!

She's loud, gregarious, and lots of fun. And I wonder if Suffield is ready for her.

"Hi Cheryl."

"So what part are you goin' for?" she asks as she sits beside me.

"Well, I don't know. I think that maybe I'll skip this one."

"You should go for the character Ben," she says.

"Why?"

"Because this part requires somebody who can perform some intense scenes."

"Oh yeah? Tell me more."

"You see," begins Cheryl, "Ben is the oldest son, and he and his father don't get along at all. The action takes place between Ben and his dad, and the interaction between the two of them can get pretty stormy. I think you'd be perfect for the part."

She's always doing this to me.

"What makes you think that?" I ask.

"Because you're a good actor," Cheryl says. "Anyway never mind that now, you seem to be a little subdued tonight. What's the matter?"

I take a deep breath. "I got laid off my job today."

"Won't they renew your contract like they always do?"

"It's permanent this time."

"Oh no," Cheryl says as she gives me a bear hug that would rival any lumberjack.

"What are you going to do now, honey?"

"I don't know. I'm thinking that this is my chance to finally move to Toronto."

"Oh don't do that honey, move out to Alberta with me," she says with a wink. "Keep me company when I'm out in the middle of nowhere."

"Hey, I'd love to," I answer. "Who knows, I just might."

Cheryl and I continue discussing my lay-off, when he walks into the theatre and looks around the auditorium.

He's tall and broad-shouldered, with short, wavy red hair, and a big, thick red moustache. He looks like he has a swimmer's build. Those blue eyes of his—they're amazingly clear and bright. And that crooked smile that he's flashing to everybody holds me in a trance.

Cheryl's voice fades to a distant echo in my ears as I concentrate on his voice. It's soft, and yet confident.

"Is this where the audition is being held?" he asks one of the guys sitting close to the exit.

The fellow he's addressing nods his head.

"Thanks," he says and walks to a seat beside the main aisle, three rows ahead of us. He glances at me and smiles, then does a double take when he sees Cheryl.

"Hi Cheryl," he says, smiling at her.

"Hi Bryn. I didn't know you were an actor."

"Oh I just dabble sometimes, and you?"

"I'm president of the theatre group, so you'd better be nice to me if you want a part."

"I'll remember that," he says. "We'll talk during break." Then he smiles at me, and nods his head, and takes his seat.

I feel the blood rush to my face. I can't take my eyes off him. I've seen a lot of good looking guys, but, *wow* is all I can say under my breath.

Cheryl leans over and whispers in my ear. "He *is* cute, isn't he?"

"What's his name?" I ask her, still dazzled by his presence.

"Bryn Menzies. He's one of our new officers just out of Royal Military College in Kingston. He's here on a course for a little while."

"How do you know him?"

"My husband introduced him to me at one of those boring formal functions at the officers' mess that we have to attend every once in a while."

Cheryl and I look at each other. "Definitely a ten," we both whisper in unison. Then we laugh.

"He's a really nice chap," Cheryl says. Then she lowers her voice and moves her face close to my ear. "And I think that he might be gay."

I smile and think, *I can only hope.*

"Well if you want I can introduce you to him during break, you two would make a great looking couple."

I laugh and in a low voice say, "You're still trying to get me a boyfriend."

"You know me, honey, always the yenta."

"The what?"

"Yenta. Oh never mind, honey, stick with me and I'll get you hitched with a nice guy."

I smile and look back to where Bryn is sitting.

"Well," says Cheryl, "I'd better get things underway." And with that, she goes to the microphone at the front of the theatre, and gets everybody in the auditorium to move closer to the stage so the audition can get started.

Maybe I'll try for the role of this Ben character just for kicks. Maybe Bryn and I'll be in the play together, and it will give me a chance to check him out.

∞

For the next hour I watch and listen as, two at a time, all interested parties take turns auditioning for various parts in the play. Chip, the director of the play, along with Cheryl and Mark, the vice-president of the troupe, sit silently, taking notes as they listen to each of us read. Every once in a while, one of them will whisper to the other in between readings. It must be difficult trying to determine who will get the various parts, but the three of them have several years experience between them.

It's Bryn's turn to read. I watch and listen to him as he auditions for the part of the father.

He told Cheryl and I that he only dabbles in live theatre, but it's clear to me that he's had a lot of training in this field. He seems to naturally take on the voice of the character he's playing. His voice has become so deep and so powerful that it seems to resound from the walls of the theatre as he reads the part of the drunk, raging, self-pitying father.

I think, *Man, I've got to get to know this guy.*

Then I'm startled back to Earth as I'm called upon to read for the part of the adversarial eldest son, Ben. I walk up to the front of the auditorium, and my heart pounds with excitement as Bryn is told to read the part of the father once more. I know this is Cheryl's doing. I look at her, and she smiles and sticks her tongue out at me.

We begin to read. I'm nervous being on stage with Bryn, but I'm trying my best to keep my cool. I glance at Cheryl every once in a while, and she has a big grin on her face making me feel even more self-conscious. After we've read for a few minutes, Chip says, "You can stop right there. I think that we've got enough to go on. Let's take a break. Okay, see everybody back here in about fifteen."

Those present in the auditorium move to the cafeteria down the hall for coffee. Jim starts the music once more, and the opening bass lines of yet another damned disco tune pounds on our eardrums.

Bryn is standing beside me, and I really want to say something to him before he goes for coffee. But I'm self-conscious. What if I open my mouth and say something stupid to him? This isn't like me. We look at each other and I smile. Then he says, "You read really well."

"You're not so bad yourself" I say, "for somebody who only dabbles in theatre."

"Okay," he laughs, "You caught me. I've done a lot of community theatre in Oshawa. The name's Bryn Menzies."

He extends his right hand to me.

"Yeah, Cheryl told me. I'm Neil Logan."

We shake hands.

"Are you going for coffee?" asks Bryn.

"Sure."

I catch the smile on Cheryl's face. She motions to me to come to her.

"Just a sec," I say to Bryn and go over to Cheryl. "You have the biggest shit-eating grin I've ever seen," she says under her breath. "Now you behave yourself."

She's right, I can't hide the grin the I'm wearing.

"You two *are* coming back to see who got the parts, aren't you?" she says with a sly smile.

"Stop it," is all that I can say. I smile, turn, and walk back to Bryn. We go up the steps of the aisle to the back door of the theatre, and out into the hallway to the cafeteria. Bryn orders two coffees, and we sit at a table in a corner.

"Judging by your haircut," says Bryn, "you're not in the Forces."

"You're right," I say running my hand through my collar-length hair. "I work on base. Or at least I did until they laid me off today."

"That must have felt like a kick in the groin. What department did you work for?"

"The Grounds Department, you know, shovelling snow, raking leaves, cleaning dog shit."

Bryn laughs and says, "A nice, clean desk job. Any plans for the future?"

"I'm gonna lay low for a couple of weeks to figure out what my next move is. I'll probably start looking for work in Toronto. "

"And if you get a part in this play?"

"I guess I'll stick around for a while, and then go to Toronto. So, Cheryl tells me that you've just arrived here from Kingston."

"Yeah, I've been at RMC for the last four years."

"What made you decide to join the forces?"

Bryn shrugs, "A few things," he says, "I wanted a university education, and I couldn't afford one on my own. I wanted a career that

I could slide into once university was finished, and I wanted a job where I could travel a lot."

Then I laugh. "Yeah, you get to travel to all of the exotic places—"

"That nobody's ever heard of," Bryn says.

We both laugh. We talk a bit about Bryn's home in Oshawa. That's where he was raised, and his parents are still there. His two older sisters got married and are raising their families there as well. Then, in what seems like no time at all, break is over and we're about to find out who got which parts. Cheryl sports a sly grin as she watches Bryn and me come back into the theatre. She shakes her finger at me as if to say, now you behave yourself. I smile and mouth the words—stop it—and take a seat beside Bryn.

Chip goes to the microphone and says, "I'd like to thank all of you for coming here tonight. All of you read really well, but as you know there are only so many parts to go around. I'm going to read out a list of names, and these are the people who I would like to stay behind. As for the rest of you, all that I can say is thank you and better luck next time."

My name is the third one that Chip calls. They've given me the part of Ben, and they gave the part of the father to a guy with a thick Newfoundland accent named Rick. Well, it looks like I won't be going to Toronto for another couple of months. I look at Bryn and think that somehow this news doesn't sadden me. Bryn didn't land a part and he looks a little disappointed.

"Hey," I say, "some of us are going to go to the mess after this. Why don't you join us?"

"No," says Bryn, "I'm kind of shy around crowds. I guess that I'm not good in groups."

"You're an actor, and you're shy around crowds?"

Bryn smiles, "I guess I just don't feel like going out tonight. Look I don't know too many people around the base, and I wouldn't mind getting to know the area. Would you mind if I called you sometime this week. Maybe you could give me a tour."

"And you're telling me that you're shy," I laugh. "Just wait here a sec."

I get up and go over to Cheryl who has a look on her face that says, *I know exactly what you're going to ask me.*

"Looking for a pen and paper are we?" She is smiling. I just smile back at her.

"You're a devil, you," she says and hands me a piece of paper, searching her purse for a pen.

I take the pen and paper, write my name and phone number on it, and thank Cheryl as I hand the pen back to her.

"Let me know when the wedding is," she says quietly while retrieving the pen.

I laugh and go back to where Bryn is standing. "Here's my number, Bryn. Give me a call."

"Thanks, I will." He folds the paper, puts it in his shirt pocket, and leaves.

∞

It's Sunday morning, and I get a phone call. It's Bryn.

"I told you I'd give you a call," he says, "How are you?"

"I'm still feeling the effects of Friday night."

"Tied one on at the mess, did you?"

"You could say that."

"Hey look, are you doing anything today?"

"No, why?"

"Wanna go for a drive? I'd like to see some of the area."

"Sure, just hang on a sec." I turn to Dad who just happens to be sitting at the kitchen table. "Dad, do you need the car today?"

He turns to Mom, "Do you need to go anywhere today?"

"No," she says, then she looks at me and smiles. "We did all of our errands yesterday, while you were hung-over."

I roll my eyes, "Thanks."

Dad shrugs and says, "I guess the car is yours today if you want it."

"Great!" I turn back to the phone. "Hey Bryn, have you been up around Wasaga Beach?"

"No."

"Why don't I come to pick you up, and we can go for a drive around there."

"I was going to come by and pick you up, but sure, that sounds great."

I jot down his barrack block number and tell him that I'll be by in about an hour. Man, he actually phoned. This is great! Any remnants of a hangover I did feel, have suddenly vanished. I finish off some small things that I was doing, have a shower, get dressed, and drive into Base. I arrive at Bryn's barrack block to see him sitting outside of the building.

I lean over and unlock the passenger door, and I don't even get a chance to say hello to him.

"You said that you were going to be here twenty minutes ago," he says with a smile on his face but scold in his voice.

I look at my watch. "I said that I'd be about an hour."

"That was about an hour and a half ago," he says sounding a bit annoyed with me.

"Oh, sorry Bryn," I say, wondering what his problem is. After a slight pause he sighs as he turns to me and says.

"No Neil, I'm sorry. I guess that I'm just a stickler for punctuality. Must be my officers' training. I'll get over it."

"No prob, bub."

We drive out of the base and head north on highway 24, toward Collingwood, which is just outside of Wasaga Beach. Our conversation is light as he tells me a little more about his family and his hometown of Oshawa.

"'Oshawitz' we call it."

I laugh. "Why?"

"Because it's a redneck town and consequently you usually feel you can't be free to express yourself," he says, "or you'll get the crap beaten out of you."

"Sort of like living on base," I say.

"You could say that. They don't like things that are different in Oshawitz."

"How do you mean 'different'?"

"Well," Bryn says, hesitating briefly, "differing points of view are viewed with, let's say, a certain amount of distrust."

Bryn looks out the window. "Anyway," he says, changing the subject, "Dad was a painter and union steward at the General Motors plant, and mom worked the assembly line. They met at a company dance. One thing led to another, and after a couple of years of dating each other, they were married."

"Do your sisters work at the plant?"

"No, one's a loans officer with the Royal Bank, and the other is a teacher. But both of my brothers-in-law work at the plant."

"You say that your sisters are older than you?"

"Yeah, I'm the youngest, the baby, the spoiled brat of the family because I'm the only son. My sisters fawn over me, I guess, to this day, they feel they have to protect me for some reason," Bryn says with a smile.

"Admit it!" I say, "You love it!"

Bryn laughs out loud. "Yeah. They were nervous when I went to New York City last summer—"

"You were in New York City?" I say excitedly.

"Yeah."

"I've always wanted to go! What was that like?"

"Well, New York isn't a city, it's an experience," Bryn says. "It was amazing. I stayed at The New York Hilton—"

"Get a load of you!" I say. "Are you sure that you still want to be seen in the same car with me?"

Bryn laughs. "Look, that city goes 24 hours a day. It just doesn't stop. The lights, the Broadway plays, I was in Heaven. Do you like musicals?"

I shrug and grunt.

"I love musicals," he says, "I must have spent a fortune trying to take in as many of them as I could while I was there."

"What was your favourite?"

Bryn thinks a bit. "It's a toss-up between Annie and A Chorus Line. But if I really had to choose between them, I'd have to say A Chorus Line was my favourite. If they ever do a tour and hit Toronto, you should go to see it. I'm sure you'd like it."

I raise my eyebrows, shrug once more, and say, "It's about an audition isn't it?"

"Yeah. You get to know all of the characters and their fears and joys. It was funny, tragic, silly, and serious. Being involved with the theatre, I'm sure that you would be able to identify with what's happening on the stage. In fact I couldn't help but think of it during the audition the other night."

We get so caught up in talking about it that before we know it we've entered Collingwood. I drive into town and take the main exit, heading east to Wasaga Beach.

Bryn starts talking like Captain Kirk on Star Trek, "So Mr. Spock what do we know about this Wasaga Beach that we're approaching?"

I laugh and play along. "Well Captain, the inhabitants call it The Longest Freshwater Beach in the World."

"Do they have good reason to call it that?"

"Apparently it stretches 14 miles along the southeast coast of Nottawasaga Bay on Lake Huron."

"Very interesting, Mr. Spock."

"I thought so, Captain."

We drive by signs introducing us to smaller beaches with names like: Bowers, Brocks and Springhurst. Each beach has its own cluster of cottages, so close together they form little villages that all connect to form one continuous rambling of streets and cottages.

25

Being early in the year, a lot of places are still boarded up. They'll finally come to life during the Easter weekend when the owners from Toronto or where ever, have their first chance to come up and breathe life into them. They'll take the boards from the windows, turn the electricity back on, cut back any weeds that have had a chance to take hold during the spring, and restock their fridges with barbecue meat and beer. We drive for miles, passing from one settlement after another, whole streets where only one or two places show signs of life inside.

I turn off the main drag and onto one of the waterfront roads. I'm surprised by what I see.

"Man, the lake's water level sure is high this spring," I comment to Bryn.

"Look at that," he says. The beach itself lies underwater. The waves gently lap the shoreline only inches from the road we're on.

"Do you think the place is sinking?" chuckles Bryn.

"Well this is the highest that I've ever seen the water level in all the years I've lived in the area," I say, not knowing what to think of this. There's no place on this narrow road to pull the car over, or I'd get out to have a closer look. We drive on to the town of Wasaga Beach, passing by empty campsites, trailer parks, and partially full motels.

We enter the town and park by the police station near a sign that indicates we're at beach area No. 2. We get out of the car and a brisk March wind off the bay slaps us. I zip up my jacket and put my hands in my pockets, so does Bryn. Wasaga Beach seems like a ghost town compared to when I'm usually here. In the summertime, this place is party central, especially for teenagers. They come from all over to party by the light of bonfires until 6am or later.

I tell Bryn how, when I was a teenager, my buddies and me would come here at least a couple of times each summer. The streets would be jam-packed with cars moving at a snail's pace and beeping their horns with their speakers blaring the likes of Led Zeppelin, Black Sabbath or the local rock radio station. We'd arrive on any July or August Friday night with sleeping bags and cases of 24 that older brothers would get for us, and party until a blanket of night would cover us.

We'd bring our girlfriends, fully intending to get them drunk and then get laid. However, more often than not, we'd pass out on the sand and wake bleary-eyed the next day with not much recollection of the night before, cursing the beer companies and nursing the pain in our heads.

Bryn and I walk down the mostly deserted streets, past the temporarily boarded shells of hot dog kiosks, fish 'n' chip joints, and souvenir stands. We pass the odd restaurant that's open for business all year around, but there doesn't seem to be too many people inside any of them at this time of the year. Huge old trees overhang the predominately deserted roads, and remnants of summers-gone-by are everywhere.

We walk by a huge wooden dance hall that sits majestically right on the beach. It's called The Dardanella—or The Dard, as we call it. It was built back in the twenties and has seen the likes of Tommy Dorsey and Glenn Miller play there in the past. It's been the place to go for summertime concerts ever since. It's a combination restaurant, lounge, pool hall and the big concert hall. Every year the management upgrades the concert hall so that we get the best sound for the big names that stop by. A bunch of us took in a couple of concerts there last summer. It's closed now, but in May when it opens again, it'll be one of *the* places to be on the entire beach right through until September.

Not too far from there sits a greasy spoon that hasn't seen an interior renovation since 1954 and still plays old Bill Haley and Elvis hits on the juke box every summer when it's open. Wasaga Beach is a combination of the way-it-was and the-way-it-is, with the only common denominator between the two being the bathing suit and tourist dollars. Bryn and I look at each other and smile silently.

"What?" I chuckle.

27

"This whole thing seems so peaceful. It's certainly a great view," he says quietly looking over the length of the beach and the lake beyond.

Just then a Golden Retriever appears out of nowhere. He sports a red collar with a tag and he approaches us as I hold out my hand to him. He sniffs it and then turns his attention to Bryn. He sniffs at Bryn and wags his tail. Bryn crouches and pets the dog. The retriever jumps up and puts both of his front paws on Bryn's shoulders, which just about knocks Bryn on his ass. The dog's tail is wagging double time, and he moves his head and front paws excitedly back and forth like he wants to play.

"He seems to really like you," I say, smiling.

"King!" yells a voice. Then around the corner of a building comes a middle aged man with a leash in his hand. The dog retreats to his owner. We exchange smiles and nod to the owner, then King takes off down the road with his master walking calmly behind him.

We continue to walk silently down the road when Bryn turns to me.

"Hungry?" he asks.

"Yeah. I could go for a munch."

"Do you know of any good places around here?"

"Yeah, there's a place down the road where we could grab lunch. We'll probably have to take the car though, it's a ways down."

"Well sure, let's go," says Bryn.

Back to the car we go and drive down the main drag until we get to a community centre. We park the car and approach the restaurant. We enter the place and sit ourselves down at a table by a window. There are only three other tables full of customers in the place, and it's warm in here compared to outside. The sun is slowly growing colder as mid-afternoon seems to rush head-long toward late-day.

A waitress appears with menus and asks us if we want anything to drink.

"No thanks," says Bryn.

I order a large Coke.

"Okay," she smiles, I'll be back in a couple of minutes to take your orders." She disappears into the kitchen.

"This is my treat," says Bryn as he opens the menu to have a look, "since you're not working right now."

"Thanks."

We both become silent. Then Bryn pipes up, "So I haven't heard you mention a girlfriend."

(I was afraid he'd eventually say something like that).

I'm a little hesitant before I answer. "I haven't had a girlfriend for about three years," I say and cast my eyes to the tabletop. "The last one, well…" Letting my thoughts wander I begin to stroke my moustache as I think about Laurie.

Bryn studies me for a bit and asks, "Did it end badly?"

I look out the window and look back to Bryn, "I was 19 and she was twenty-five."

"You go for the older women, eh?" he says with a smirk.

I manage a slight smile. "I guess. Laurie and I had a pretty good thing goin', until I got her pregnant."

"Ahh," Bryn says as if a suspicion has just been confirmed.

I inhale slowly. "Yep, mom panicked. Dad wanted me to 'do-the-honourable-thing' and marry her—"

"You weren't into that?"

"Hell no. I wasn't ready for that." I sigh. "But I was with Laurie the whole time that she was pregnant, Christ knows that I felt I should stick around. But as soon as she had the kid, she told me to fuck off and then moved away."

"Have you heard from her since?"

"No. All I know is that I have a three year old son living some-where around St. Catharines."

The waitress appears with my Coke. "Are you ready to order?" she asks as she sets my drink on the table.

"Actually," says Bryn, "not yet."

"That's okay. I'll come back in a couple of minutes."

"Oh," Bryn motions to the waitress as she turns to go, "I've changed my mind, could you bring me a large Coke after all?"

"Sure," she says.

"Oh, by the way," I say to the waitress.

"Yes?"

"We noticed on the way in that the water level in the bay looks really high this year. Do you know why that is?"

"Melt water."

"Melt water?"

"Yeah," she smiles, "this happens every year when the ice on the lake melts."

"Oh."

She smiles and returns to the bar.

"Melt water," I say to Bryn feeling a little stupid for not thinking of the obvious.

"Do you think that you might see your son some day?"

"I doubt it."

"Do you know his name?"

"Aaron. She named him after her father."

The waitress reappears with Bryn's Coke. Then, both of us feeling stupid for not deciding on an order yet, quickly scan the menu. We make a snap decision, and order the same hamburger deluxe. The waitress smiles and says, "Oh this is an easy order. Thanks." She collects the menus and heads into the kitchen.

Bryn and I are alone again, for the next few minutes anyway. Our eyes meet and lock for a few seconds. We break the temporary spell by looking away from each other at the same time.

I feel like he's looked directly into the deepest, darkest part of me and has seen what makes me tick. It makes me feel vulnerable. I get this feeling that he'd like to tell me something, and I'd like to think that it would be to tell me he's gay. I suddenly feel uncomfortable, and I sense that he is too.

"Ah shit!" I find myself saying aloud as some disco music comes blaring at us through the jukebox.

"What?" asks Bryn.

I point at the jukebox, "That shit that they've got playin'."

Bryn laughs, "You don't like disco?"

"I *hate* this fuckin' shit!"

To deliberately annoy me Bryn starts to sign along with the song, "We're going to Boogie, Oogie, Oogie, till we just can't boogie no more."

"You know where the hell you can go!" I say trying to hide the smile that's drawing across my face as I watch him. "I suppose that you like this shit."

Bryn laughs, "I don't mind it. It's great fun sometimes."

A shudder runs through my body like I've just had a mouthful of raw liver. Bryn continues to laugh at me.

"I suppose you got a whole collection of this shit," I say, half-jokingly.

"I like all kinds of music," says Bryn when he finally settles down from laughing, "But no, I've got no disco in my collection."

"Well that's a relief." Then, changing the subject, I ask him about his past loves.

"The last girlfriend I had was when I was in Kingston," he says. "It only lasted a couple of months. We had great sex, but the relationship never really went any further than that."

"So the relationship was just sex?"

"Yeah, but no. I liked her quite a bit, but I knew that I wouldn't be sticking around for very long, so I didn't want any kind of commitment at the time."

"How did she react to you leaving?"

"She didn't. I told her that I was being posted to Borden, and she told me that it'd been a slice. So we got into bed, had some wild sex and then we went out for dinner and said goodbye."

"Just like that?"

"Just like that," he says. "It was just as well. As it turns out neither of us wanted anything serious at the time."

The waitress appears and lays two platters with hamburgers and fries with small sides of cole slaw in front of us.

"Would you guys like refills on the Cokes?" she asks.

That's a yes from me and a no from Bryn. We dig into our food, when she disappears once more. We eat in silence.

Our platters are finally empty, and I polish-off the last of my second Coke while Bryn's first glass is still half-full. I stare out the window at the parking lot and the submerged beach beyond. The late afternoon sun is low on the horizon, and soon it will be dark. I don't like to drive at night, so I'm thinking that maybe we should leave soon. A steady stream of disco has slapped us from the jukebox all through the meal. I might have to take some Pepto-Bismol to settle my stomach when I get home—disco just affects me like that.

I look back at Bryn, who's looking at me. He gives me a crooked smile. "Where are you, guy?"

"Captain, I'm thinking that we should be heading back to Star base shortly."

"I think you're right, Mr. Spock."

We get the waitress to bring us the bill and Bryn pays. We put on our coats go back out to the car, and head back to the Base.

∞

As I lie in bed, staring at the ceiling, the faint glow of the neighbour's porch light illuminates my walls and casts a weird glow on things around the room. My blue denim shirt hanging off of my desk chair looks white, and the red t-shirt strewn across the end of my bed looks grey.

It's already been a month since Bryn and I spent that afternoon at Wasaga Beach. I look back at the ceiling and think about how I've been feeling this last month. I don't know what's been wrong with me. I've been almost totally preoccupied with Bryn. Try as I might, I just can't seem to get him out of my mind. A lot of times he'll show up at rehearsal, and I really find it hard to concentrate when he's around. It's like I'm aware that he's watching me, and I'll forget my lines and get really clumsy on-stage. Sometimes I have to mentally slap myself to bring me out of this state of mind. I just don't understand what's going on.

He's been giving me all of the signals that he's interested in me because sometimes when we're alone, our eyes will lock and he'll give me a look that seems to say, I know what you want, and I want it too. Then he'll wink at me, and I'll smile back at him.

So tonight something's happened between Bryn and I that really has me going. We went into Barrie to see that new Woody Allen movie, *Interiors*. It's really different for Woody Allen, it's dramatic rather than funny. Anyway, on our way back, he invited me to his room at the barrack block for a drink.

We got into his room and Bryn sat on his bed, while I settled into an armchair facing him.

I swore that this particular evening I would tell him how I've been feeling about him. I had wanted to tell him for so long that now was the time to say something.

He got up and put his favourite album on his turntable, *Aja* by Steely Dan, then took out a bottle of red wine that he had stashed in his closet. Using his Swiss Army knife, he uncorked it and brought out a couple of water glasses.

"I didn't think that you guys were allowed to have booze in your rooms, I said to him.

He smiled and pressed his index finger to his mouth in a shhh motion.

"These aren't exactly fine crystal," he smiled as he handed me a glass, "But I didn't think you'd mind that."

"Hell no."

He poured a couple of glasses, and handed one to me.

"Bryn," I said, working up my courage, "I've got something to tell you."

"Yeah?" he said. And there was a pregnant pause between us.

"I like you. In fact, I really like you. If you get my drift."

He looked at me and gave me that crooked smile. "I guess I knew that," he said, "every time I look at you, you're looking at me."

The two of us smiled in nervous silence, and I just couldn't tear my gaze from his.

"The truth is," Bryn confessed, "I like you as well."

"I guess I knew that, too," I said.

He smiled and glanced at the floor then returned his gaze to me. "You know, I don't think I've ever felt this way about a guy before." Then he fidgeted nervously with his glass.

My heart raced as I pulled the chair I was sitting on over directly in front of him. I gently put my hands on his shoulders and let my fingers slowly knead the flesh on the back of his neck and shoulders. He let his head slowly roll forward. I put my face in his hair and gently rubbed it along the top of his head. He didn't resist.

I continued to massage the back of his neck, and then I felt Bryn's body lean into mine. My massaging slowly became caressing, and the two of us put our arms completely around each other. Bryn completely leaned into me. He moved his head up, put it on my shoulder, and shut his eyes. I continued to caress the back of his neck and shoulders.

He raised his head from my shoulder, opened his eyes, put his hands on either side of my face. I put my arms around his neck, and I felt him resist me a bit.

"Give it up, Bryn," I whispered to him as I moved my face closer to his.

We kissed. We kissed again. Then we gently put our lips together and opened our mouths to kiss deeply, letting our tongues taste each other. A moan escaped Bryn's mouth as I sucked on his tongue. The warmth of his breath with mine and the taste of his tongue in my mouth was more than I could stand. With his tongue still in my mouth, my hands slowly undid the top buttons on his shirt. Bryn did nothing.

I spread the fabric of Bryn's shirt to reveal his hairless chest. I gently put my hand on his firm, tender flesh and ran my hand along its expanse. Bryn watched my hands as I caressed him. I moved my face to his chest where I could smell the scent of his skin; I could feel the heat from his body and the excited pulse of his veins. I felt his heart rapidly beating; his breathing grew heavier. He put his right hand on the back of my head.

I ran my tongue over his chest and could taste the salt of his flesh. Then I licked at one of his nipples. He moaned once more. I slowly ran my hand down his leg and gently cupped his crotch, then I began to squeeze.

"No," he said, in a hoarse whisper. There was a hint of panic in his voice as he took my hand from his crotch. He almost darted straight up on his bed. "No, not now."

I shut my eyes and nodded my head in silence, still reeling from this slap back to Earth.

"Look, it's almost 10 o'clock," he said nervously getting off of the bed and doing his shirt back up, "Maybe I should drive you home now."

"Okay," I said, disappointed.

Bryn said nothing as we put on our shoes and jackets.

"Bryn, are you okay?"

He answered without looking at me. "Yeah." Then he turned to me. "Sorry Neil. I'm just not sure that I'm ready for the sex thing yet," he said with a slight panic in his voice.

"That's understandable," I said, though I didn't understand.

"Are you ready to go?" he asked.

I nodded my head.

Bryn locked the door to his room and we walked to his vehicle, a light blue 1979 Renault Le Car. When we finally stopped in front of my parents' place, he turned to me and said, "Look, I'm sorry about the sex thing."

"That's okay," I said, though again it didn't feel okay. "When you're ready, alright?"

He said nothing but quickly added, "Look, there's a formal party taking place at the Officers' Mess next weekend that I have to attend, and I'm allowed to bring a guest. I'd like you to come along."

This statement startled me. "Are you sure you want me along?"

"Look Neil, I'd really like you to come along, okay? It's a formal thing, you'll have to wear a jacket and tie. Besides, it'll give you a chance to see a little of my world."

This intrigued me, and I agreed to attend. He said that he would give me a call in a couple of days and fill me in on the details. I got out of the car and watched him disappear into the night.

∞

I'm wearing a black, three-piece suit, with a conservative tie and a white shirt. I think, *this'll really knock him out.* But when he shows up, it's me who's totally blown away. It's the first time that I've seen him in his formal uniform, and that only seems to accentuate his good looks. We go to this gathering, and on the way there Bryn tells me that he's expected to spend a lot of the time talking with other officers. He asks me if I would mind, and I tell him not to worry about it.

"By the way you're looking very handsome tonight," Bryn says to me as we drive Le Car—we've taken to calling it Le Car—into the parking lot of the Building.

"Thanks. I'm knocked out by seeing you in uniform."

A huge smile lights his face. "Thank you," he says.

He parks the car, and as we're walking across the parking lot I say, "I have to admit I'm a little nervous about this. I hope everything goes well."

"Don't worry about it," Bryn says, "you're a good actor."

"Jeez thanks," I say, not knowing whether to take that as a compliment or not.

Bryn laughs and winks at me as we enter the Officers' Mess.

I mingle with everybody there, and I feel confident I'm able to hold my own with this "oh-so-tasteful" crowd. The one person who really seems interested in talking with me happens to be Bryn's Commanding Officer. If this was a gay bar in Toronto, I'd swear that he was cruising me. He says he's interested in live theatre, and recognizes me from the Little Theatre's last production. He seems to be very interested in what I have to say and doesn't seem to want to let me talk with anybody else. We talk about the troupe's past performances and plans for upcoming plays. Every once in a while he smiles and winks at me. That makes me feel a bit uncomfortable because I'm not sure what that's supposed to mean—not with this crowd anyway. Because he's Bryn's Commanding Officer, and to be polite, I just smile at him whenever he does that.

At one point during our long conversation, I catch Bryn looking at me from across the room. He's in a small group of people involved in a lively and animated conversation about what seems to be politics. Like a small boy playing hide-and-seek, he peeks around the shoulder of one of the people in the group he's part of, smiles, raises his glass and winks at me. Now I've got two guys in uniform winking at me—too much.

When the evening is over, Bryn and I get in Le Car and laugh all the way back to my place. Bryn brings the car to a stop in front of my house. Except for the lonely vigil the front porch light keeps against the wee-hours-of-the-morning, all of the lights in the house are out. In fact every light in every house on the street is out.

I undo my seatbelt and lift the door handle to get out of the car.

"No," says Bryn, "Stay here a minute, I wanna talk."

I let go of the door handle, and turn to look at him.

Bryn shuts off the ignition and says, "I really like you Neil, I want you to know that. I'm proud of the way that you handled yourself tonight, especially with my C.O.

"I think your C.O. might be gay, I had the feeling he was cruising me."

Bryn laughs and says, "Rumour has it that's the case. I won't say anything if you don't."

"I know nothing!" I mimic Sergeant Schultz from the '60s TV show Hogan's Heroes.

Then he looks me in the eye, smiles, and says, "I want you to know I, well, that I'm growing very fond of you."

He gives me that crooked smile of his. "I get a kick out you, Neil. I can't explain what it is, but you make me feel so, I don't know, so alive." He puts his hand on my cheek. Then, looking a little nervous and breaking the spell he says, "I gotta get back to barracks."

"Okay," I say. "Thanks, Bryn. I had a good time tonight."

"Me too," he says.

I reluctantly get out of his car and watch as he drives up the street and turns out of my sight. In the balmy spring darkness, I stand in the lone light of the streetlamp.

I feel like hollering, jumping, dancing, and singing like in the old movie musicals when the guy gets the girl and breaks into some corny song and dance routine. I can't help it. It's just the way that I'm feeling. I can't remember ever feeling this free!

∞

It's a Saturday afternoon in late May, and I'm lazing in the backyard with Frank. I'm sporting nothing but my sunglasses and cutoffs, enjoying the sun. A half-full bottle of beer rests on the ground at my feet. We sit quietly, listening to music from a portable radio on the ground in front of us.

I'm thinking about my life and of all of the changes that have happened to me over the last couple of months. A month ago, Pete managed to score me a temporary job washing dishes at the same mess hall as him. It will only last until the end of next month, and I don't mind the work. The pay's not bad, and it'll give me some extra cash to stash away for my eventual move to Toronto.

The theatre company performed Leaving Home two weeks ago, and after six weeks of rehearsing, it was a success! Three nights of packed houses, and the audiences loved it. The climax of the play was when Ben and his father have another of their emotionally charged arguments, and Ben's dad beats him with his belt. Ben takes his packed suitcase and storms out of the house.

Luckily for me, that scene is almost near the end of the play and I didn't make another appearance on-stage after that. When I performed it, I would usually take about five minutes to calm down from all of the emotion on-stage.

At the end of the play, when we were all taking our bows, Rick, the actor who played Ben's dad, and I would shake hands. We'd get standing ovations when that happened. Bryn came to see the final performance, and the both of us went to the cast party at Chip's place afterward. So because Bryn and I arrived together, Cheryl kidded me about it all night.

She'd whisper things to me like, "Well it looks like we'll have to go into Toronto to get a wedding dress for ya." She's too much sometimes.

And speaking about Bryn, we've been getting to know each other really well over the last month and a half. It feels like we've become quite close really fast. He's been over to the house a couple of Saturdays to have dinner and watch the hockey game on TV. My family all think that he's great, and that's important to me. Dad and him talk about the military when he's here, and mom makes comments to me about how handsome he is. The only comment that Frank says about Bryn is, "he's a good shit." Pete, well he doesn't really say anything because he's usually in his room with the record player on, whether Bryn's here or not.

Just about every weekend we've done something together. We went camping a couple of weekends ago, and last weekend we spent a day together in Toronto. But damn, we still haven't had sex. The closest that we got was that night in Bryn's room at his barrack block, a couple of months back. He says that he still isn't ready for the sex thing yet. I guess that I can understand that. After all, it was only a couple of years ago that I was feeling the same way that he is.

I remember trying to come to terms with this whole gay thing. Not being sure of where I was sexually left me feeling confused a lot of the time. Many times I would be in bed with Laurie and thinking about some guy that I had seen. Then I would feel guilty. I'd feel like a scumbag and hate myself. It's taken me quite a while to get comfortable feeling this way about other guys, so I guess I can understand what Bryn must be going through.

Because of what I'm feeling for Bryn, I now have mixed feelings about moving to Toronto. Don't get me wrong, it's still in the back of my mind, but now with Bryn around—shit, I've kicked over what's left of my beer! Frank laughs.

"Asshole," he says smiling, "you've wasted what's left of a perfectly good beer."

"Fuck off," is the only comeback that I can think of.

As the end of the song on the radio begins to fade, the news announcer barges in, *"This is the news at the top of the hour. More on the gay riots in San Francisco last night…"*

I go over and turn up the radio.

"…As we've been reporting, the San Francisco gay community went on a rampage last night as former city supervisor Dan White was given a seven year eight month sentence for the murders of Mayor George Muscone, and openly gay supervisor Harvey Milk. Five thousand angry gays and lesbians converged on San Francisco City Hall, and it is estimated that 300 people, including 60 policemen were injured during the confrontation. Thirteen police cruisers were destroyed by fire, and damage is estimated at over one million—"

"They should've hung that bastard!" I spit. "He fuckin' well planned those murders."

"I'm with you," says Frank.

Mom calls me from the kitchen window, "Neil! Telephone! It's Bryn!"

I leave the scene of the beer mishap, picking up the spilt bottle along the way, sprint into the kitchen, and pick up the receiver.

"Hey Bryn."

"Hi Neil. How are you?"

"I was just in the back yard takin' in some sun."

"Look Neil, I'd like to see you. Are you busy right now?"

"No plans."

"Good, do you want to go into Barrie for a pizza? There's something that I want to talk to you about."

"Sure. What's up?"

"I want to save it until we get into town. Can you be ready in about fifteen minutes?"

"Ah, sure."

"Great. See you then."

I go to my room and put on a pair of jeans and a t-shirt with *Fleetwood Mac* emblazoned across the front of it. I go to the front door and wait because when Bryn says he'll be along in fifteen minutes, he means it.

"Hey mom," I say to her as she sits on the sofa knitting.

"Mmhm?"

"I'm going into Barrie with Bryn. He wants to talk. I'm going to be grabbing a bite to eat with him."

"Are you leaving now?"

"I'm just waiting for him to arrive."

"Well, see you when you get back."

Bryn shows up almost exactly fifteen minutes later, and he's got a huge grin on his face as I get into the car. I grin back at him and shake my head. "Okay tell me," I say.

"Wait until we get there." He continues to grin.

I shrug my shoulders while raising my eyebrows. "Okay, you win."

As we drive out of Angus, I notice that Bryn keeps glancing at me.

"Are you growing a beard?" he asks.

"Yeah, just for the hell of it."

"So far, so good," he says. "I think it'll look good on you."

"Thanks, Bryn." And suddenly I can feel myself swell with pride.

All the way into Barrie, we listen to Bryn's favourite Steely Dan tape on the car stereo. I direct him to a pizza place I haven't been to in a while. As I recall, the food wasn't bad. In what seems like an instant, we're sitting in a black-walled, dimly-lit tacky Spanish-style pizza place. Red velvet paintings of Matadors and Galleons are alternately hung between the fake swords and shields mounted on the black wooden backboards. As I look around, I can see that there have been a few changes made to the place since I was here last.

A small dance floor has been installed in the centre of the room. A disco floor in a pizza joint—hell, what next—the constant motion of the reflections of a small, mirrored ball in the centre of the ceiling, above the dance floor, swirls around the width of the dance area. We both order beers and they arrive at our table almost instantly.

A jukebox used to blink hypnotically in the darkened corner by the exit door, adjacent to the new dance floor. I could play songs from rock bands like Fleetwood Mac, Steve Miller, Thin Lizzy, and Boston. But now the management has decided to get on the obnoxious disco bandwagon, and that's what ricochets off the dance floor from the small speakers suspended above it. At least the volume of the music is somewhat low so we can hear ourselves talk.

"So, are you going to tell me this exciting news that you have for me or what?" I say with a wide smile as I'm pouring the beer from the bottle to a mug.

Bryn still has that big, shit-eating grin, "I've been posted to Calgary," he says with a gleam in his eyes.

"Oh," is the only response that I can muster as I finish pouring my beer.

"I've got to be there by mid-July," he says with an excited tone in his voice.

"Well Bryn, I guess that congratulations are in order," I say reluctantly raising my mug to him.

"Thanks," says Bryn as we clink our beer mugs together and have a swallow. Inside I feel like the air has been sucked from out of me. I'm smiling at him, but I'm feeling lonely already.

I lean toward Bryn and say, "You know I'm going to miss the hell out of you when you're gone." Then I raise the mug to my mouth to have another swallow.

"Look," Bryn says, "Why don't you come out west with me?"

I stop short of bringing the beer mug to my mouth and momentarily stare at him motionless.

He laughs. "You should see the look on your face!"

I put my mug back down on the table. I manage a grin and look down to my mug. Then I look across the table to him.

"Are you serious?"

He grins. "Look Neil, it would be great. We could take turns driving and I could use the company. Besides, Calgary's booming right now. You could probably get a decent job there no problem."

It occurs to me that Bryn is absolutely right. There aren't any permanent job opportunities in this area; the most that I can hope for here is seasonal work. And the situation in Toronto is not all that hot right now either. A lot of the people that I know in Toronto are on Unemployment Insurance.

I'm silent. A million thoughts come at me from all directions.

"Calgary," I say. "I've never thought of moving to another province."

"We could camp along the way." Bryn adds.

Hmmm, Calgary, I think as if in a daydream.

Then I look at Bryn, smile, and say, "Wow, I'm going to have to give this some thought."

"Okay Neil, think about it. But look, I think your choice is obvious. What future prospects do you have here?"

"My family's here."

"Fair enough, but what about a permanent job? I don't think you want to live in Angus for the next twenty years."

"You know that."

He smiles at me, then reaches across the table to give my arm a gentle shake. "Go west young man," he says. "Think of it as a new adventure."

We spend the rest of the evening drinking a couple of beer, eating a large salami, green pepper, and bacon pizza, and talking about Calgary. Bryn's never been there, and he's looking forward to being out west for a couple of years. Me, I've never been out west, and I sure like the idea of an adventure.

There's one last piece of pizza left on the tray and, almost as if rehearsed, Bryn and I reach for it and our hands collide. We lock eyes for an instant while both of us sport grins that say, *I know what you're thinking.* I move my hand back and let Bryn take the last piece.

"Well," I say trying to quickly break the spell, "I've got enough money stashed away to last me about a month—"

"And you'll have a full time job by the time that your money is exhausted," says Bryn. "The economy is booming out there right now. You've got no choice," he says with a wink. "You have to come to Calgary with me."

I'm tickled by what Bryn's saying. Listening to him has hit me in all the right places. I laugh. I just laugh.

∞

Later that evening, we arrive back in Angus; he drops me off outside the house, and continues on to the Base. I go inside and after removing my shoes I walk past the living room where my parents are watching TV.

"How was your evening with Bryn?" asks Dad as he and Mom stare into the TV as if hypnotized by the electric blue light of a re-run of *The Beachcombers.*

"Great," I say as I go to the kitchen. I grab a clean glass from the cupboard above the sink, and pour myself some water from the tap. I turn away from the sink and lean against the counter beside it. Glass of water in my right hand, I fold my arms and stare into space letting my mind wander. I'm suddenly aware of my father entering the kitchen.

"You look like the cat whose swallowed the canary," he says with a huge grin.

I laugh.

"You know something that I don't know?" He asks.

"I guess I do, Dad. There 's something I have to tell you."

"What's that?" he says as he turns on the water faucet to fill the teakettle.

"I'm moving to Calgary."

The water runs from the faucet as my father stops what he's doing as if in a temporary state of suspended animation. Then, back still turned to me he says, "Calgary's a hell of a long way from Toronto. What's brought on this change of heart?"

"Bryn's been posted there. He'll be driving out, and he wants me to share the driving duties. That's why he wanted to see me tonight."

"Well," says dad, "the job prospects are certainly better in Alberta than they are in Ontario right now. This'll be a new adventure for you."

"That's what Bryn said. I guess that it makes a lot of sense in so many ways for me to go. I just never thought of moving almost to the other side of the country."

"When does Bryn have to report for duty?"

"Mid-July, but we figure that we should be there for the beginning of the month. It'll give us time to find a place to rent."

"You two are going to share a place?"

"Yeah, once we get a place and get settled in, we hope that we have a little time to get to know the city."

"Where are you guys going to stay until you've found a place off the base?"

"Well, I guess we haven't given that much thought. Bryn will probably stay at the barracks and I'll probably get a room at the Y until we rent a place. I guess that we'll have to talk about that a little more."

Dad cocks an eyebrow at me sceptically, and then puts the filled kettle on the stove.

Just then the phone rings, and I answer.

"Hello."

"Hello. Is Neil there?"

"That's me."

"Hello Neil, it's Wilf."

"Wilf!" I say excitedly, "How are ya doin'?" I watch my father as he gives me a smile and then leaves the kitchen.

"I feel great! And you?"

"Life is good!"

"I'm actually surprised to find you're still in Angus. I thought that you would have moved to Toronto by now like you've talked about."

"Well as a matter of fact, I am about to make a move to Calgary."

"Calgary? When are you moving there?"

"Last week in June. The guy that I'm driving with is in the forces and has to report for duty the middle of July."

I can hear my parents going at it again in the living room.

—but he doesn't know anybody in Calgary.

—there you go again woman.

—Don't 'there-you-go-again' me, I'll say what I think. Why do you have to argue with everything I say?

—I don't argue with everything you say.

I cover one ear so I can hear Wilf better.

"Are you still there, Neil?"

"Yeah, sorry I got a bit distracted."

"So do either of you know anybody who lives in Calgary?"

"No."

"Well you do now, actually," says Wilf.

"Oh?"

"Yep. I was just talking to Nick this afternoon. You two will be neighbours. He's landed a job in Calgary." "No shit!" I say.

"Yeah, he'll be out there by early July."

"That's too much. What kind of a job did he get?"

46

"Shipper/receiver for some trucking company out there. He's already been out to Calgary and has a house for the family to move into."

"Fantastic!"

"Maybe you can stay with him for a while until you get yourself settled."

"Hmm, that's a possibility."

"Anyway, the reason I'm phoning is to invite you to our farewell barbeque on June 23rd. Aggie and I have sold the house, so we're off to live in British Columbia after the August long weekend. Although at this point it looks like this is going to be a going away party for you and Nick as well."

I laugh. "Well it looks like I'll have to be there then."

"That's right, so bring whatever you're going to drink and something to put on the barbeque. Arrive anytime after three in the afternoon. You have my address, don't you?"

"Yeah I do, right outside of the thriving metropolis of Alliston."

"Smart-ass," Wilf says. "So we'll see you on June 23rd."

"You bet."

"Bye for now."

"See you then, Wilf."

I leave the kitchen just as the kettle begins to whistle, go into my bedroom, close the door, and turn on the radio. I lie on the bed with my arms folded behind my head and stare at the ceiling. This whole idea hasn't quite sunk in yet. *Calgary,* I think, *Nick's moving to Calgary.* A smile draws across my lips. *Man this is too much. I wonder what it's like to live there. I wonder what the gay scene is like?* I reach under my bed and grab the small stack of magazines that I keep hidden from view.

I know that I've seen them before, I think as I madly rifle through the various examples of gay political and soft porn magazines: Blueboy, In Touch, Mandate, ah here it is: The Body Politic. I pick it out and flip through the pages of a couple of editions until I find them: The Community Listings. The Body Politic publishes the addresses and phone numbers of all the gay and lesbian organizations across

Canada. I look up Calgary—not bad, they seem to have quite a few resources there. Who'd of thought, back at Christmas, that I'd be about to move to another province at the end of June. I'll be living there in only a few weeks!

∞

I drive through the main gate of the Base and take the main road through Borden and then out of the southern exit of Borden to Alliston. I sing along with the radio as The Doobie Brothers sing, *Minute by Minute*, and I make the short trek to the sleepy town and Wilf's going away party.

I hear that Alliston probably won't be sleepy for very much longer. Rumour has it there's a plan to build a Honda car plant here. At least that'll finally bring some steady jobs to the area rather than the unending seasonal work that we've all endured over the years. If the rumours are true, I can't wait to see Alliston in the next ten years, it'll be a totally different place.

Bryn's gone down to Oshawa to visit his family for the week, so I won't be seeing him again until the morning that we leave—and that's only next week! Where's the time gone? It seems like just last week that he asked me to go out west with him.

I drive to Wilf and Aggie's place. I stop the car and take the beer and steak that I brought for the barbeque from the passenger seat, then I get out and approach the house.

I walk through the wooden gate which is propped open with a hockey stick handle. It has a Wet Paint sign tacked to it. A modest white painted, frame house beckons me as I pass a For Sale sign staked on the front lawn with Sold stuck diagonally across it. As I make my way to the front steps, the sound of laughter, music, and excited chatter pour through the screen door and the living room windows like water frothing over the spillway of a dam. I arrive at the door and look through the window to see a living room full of people, faces that I don't recognize.

I knock, and in an instant Wilf answers.

"Neil, I'm so glad that you could make it!"

"Hey, I wouldn't miss this."

"C'mon in."

I enter the small vestibule and kneel to untie my shoes.

"Don't worry about your shoes," says Wilf. "C'mon through." So I follow him into the crowded, din-filled living room, case of beer in hand. The late afternoon sun streams through the window and dances around the room, almost blinding me to the dozen-or-so faces that have suddenly turned their attention to me.

"I'll take those," says Wilf as I hand him my things.

"Everyone," says Wilf addressing the mostly white-haired crowd. "I worked with this handsome young gent on the base. His name is Neil, and you'll all have to introduce yourselves to him." Then he turns back to me and asks, "Do you want a cold beer?"

"That sounds good to me."

"I'll be right back," Wilf says as he takes my beer and steak to the kitchen, "I'll tell Aggie that you're here."

"Well, I recognize this fine young gentleman," I hear a voice from the crowd in the living room say. It's old Len the gatekeeper on base.

"How are you, Len?" I ask excitedly as I extend my hand to him.

"Never in my life have I had a better day," comes that response that I've always loved to hear.

"Neil, this is the good-wife, Grace."

Grace and I shake hands and exchange pleasantries.

"So young fella," says Len with a smile, "I understand that you're on your way to Calgary."

"Wow, everybody knows," I say.

Len laughs. "Yes, this isn't a very big community."

"Yeah, I'm heading to Calgary. I can hardly believe it myself."

"Have you ever been to Calgary before?" Grace asks.

"No," I say, "and I really don't know what to expect."

"Oh I think you'll like it," says Grace softly. "The prairies are wonderful. You know what they say, 'Go west young man.'"

I laugh and say, "Yeah. I'm looking forward to—"

"Welfert says that handsome Neil Logan's in the living room!" bellows a voice from the kitchen. Into the living room walks Aggie. Aggie is a petite woman, measuring all of five foot nothing. A farm girl who's grown up in rural Ontario, Aggie never talks to you as much as she barks at you. She's entertaining, especially with that rural Ontario twang in her voice. It makes her speak in an almost hillbilly-like way. She walks over to me, gives me a hug and then hands me a cold beer.

"So I hear you're gonna go out to Calgary to break a few hearts!"

I laugh.

"I always said that if I was a few years younger," she says addressing the crowd, "this young man would be in big trouble."

Several chuckles from some of the women ricochet around the room, and I feel embarrassed.

"Oh he's twice as handsome when he turns red," says one of the other women in the room. Now I really don't know what to say or do. I just don't handle compliments very well.

"Leave the poor guy alone," smiles Wilf as he winks at me. "C'mon Neil, there's some folks in the yard that you'll want to see."

"Nice meeting everybody," I say as I exit with Wilf.

We go through to the back yard. Two barbeques stand at attention to my right as I exit the house onto the patio. They sizzle, as they'll soon be ready to give up their bounty of hot dogs, hamburgers, steaks, and chicken legs. Two men that I don't recognize, beer and cooking utensils in hand, chat about the upcoming CFL season while keeping watch over the sizzling food. I give a nod of a hello to them as Wilf and I pass. They stop their conversation just long enough to return my hellos.

A large table stretches across the left side of the patio, dressed in a large brightly coloured plastic tablecloth, and laden with an assortment of brightly coloured bowls and baskets containing everything from potato salad to hamburgers buns.

As I follow Wilf across the patio and down the steps into the yard, the first person that I see is Nick. He's sitting on a patio chair, talking with several other people, while his wife, Sylvie, sits beside him gently rocking their baby daughter, Rhiann, in a small blue stroller. Above the murmur of the adults, I can hear the squeal of small children as they swarm around Wilf's yard playing a game of Star Wars.

"Hey Nick," I say as I extend my hand to him.

Nick's face lights up as he sees me. "I was told that you were going to be here," he says as we shake hands.

"Well I guess that this is just as much our going-away party as it is Wilf and Aggie's," I smile as I hear myself say that.

"Yeah, Wilf told me that you're heading out to Calgary."

"I guess this means we're gonna be neighbours."

"I suppose so. Oh by the way," says Nick turning his attention to his wife, "you remember my wife, Sylvie?"

Sylvie smiles, "Hi Neil, how have you been?"

"Excited," I say as I grab a patio chair and sit down, "with this upcoming move to Calgary."

"I can understand that," she says, "we're feeling that way ourselves. I've never been out west, so I'm looking forward to this. When Nick got laid off, we were disappointed that we weren't going camping in Algonquin Park. So it looks like we'll be going camping this year after all, in the Rockies."

"Yeah," I say, "I'm looking forward to going out west. I understand that you're supposed to be leaving really soon."

"Nick starts work in the middle of July," Sylvie says, "so the movers will be here next week."

"When are you going to be there?" Nick asks me.

"Well we're leaving in about a week and hopefully we'll arrive in Calgary just after the July first weekend."

"We?" asks Nick looking a bit confused.

"The guy I'm driving with is in the Forces, and he's been posted to Calgary."

"Which guy is that?"

"I know him through the theatre group on the base."

"Ah," says Nick, "Are you going to be staying with anybody when you arrive?"

"No, I'll probably be staying at the Y while Bryn stays in barracks. Then we might room together. You know, rent a place off Base."

"You're welcome to stay with us until you get settled," says Sylvie, "if you don't mind noisy kids."

"Yeah," says Nick, "give us a call, and stay with us. I'll give you our address and phone number in Calgary before we leave tonight."

"Thanks that would be great, and no I don't mind kids at all."

"So are you guys going through the States?" asks Sylvie.

"No, we're driving to Kapuskasing. and we'll camp around there. Then the next day we'll drive to Thunder Bay, then we're going to make a stop in Winnipeg for a couple of days to see some friends of mine. Then we head to Calgary."

At that moment, Art appears on the patio with his wife, Peg. I watch Wilf as he moves quickly to the patio and chats with the two of them, and then Johnny appears from the house clutching a bottle of beer.

"Uh oh, look whose just arrived," I say to Nick as I point at Art.

Nick turns toward the patio he smiles and shouts, "Okay, everyone the party's over, we can all go home now!"

Art laughs, shakes his head and points at Nick, "And you know where you can go!"

Art's two young daughters race ahead of them as they come down the patio stairs to join the swarm of noisy kids running like a giant flock of pigeons from one corner of the yard to the other. Squeals of delight blend with kid-made sound effects and the occasional crying because of a skinned knee. It's amazing that any of us can hear ourselves talk over the noise. I can only catch snippets of what the kids are yelling to each other as they zip by us like noisy flying insects.—Mommy! Look at me!

—I'm Luke Skywalker!

—You're not playing fair!

—Chewbacca doesn't sound like that, he sounds like this!

"Now don't get your dresses dirty or there'll be trouble!" warns Peg as the two girls disappear into the noisy, restless whirlpool of kids.

Art, Peg, and Johnny join us as the circle of lawn chairs we're sitting in continues to grow. In his almost constant nervousness, Johnny spills his entire beer down the front of him as he sits down. He leaps to attention shouting, "Oh! Oh! Oh! Oh!" as he runs around like his shirt was on fire.

Art's daughters laugh at him and then call to Johnny to play Star Wars with them. That's it. Johnny, being the world's biggest kid, can't resist and he's off playing with the hornets' nest of kids, quickly forgetting about his beer-soaked shirt, declaring to the kids that he's Darth Vader and immediately lunges toward them. They squeal in delight, laugh, and scatter while he chases them.

Art, Peg, and I laugh at this sight, along with a few others in the circle of lawn chairs.

"So," Art says to me while he lights a cigarette, "Wilf tells me you're heading to Alberta like Nick is."

"Yeah, I guess that's where the jobs are now. How about you? Are you gonna make the horses a full-time thing?"

"At this point I'm gonna have to. I've hired Johnny to help me out. He's good with the horses."

We all look over to Johnny, who has now been wrestled to the ground by the swarm of children and continues to claim, "Darth Vader cannot be beaten!" We all laugh.

"Besides," continues Art, "we'll be making a trip to the Calgary Stampede this year, so we might be seeing you."

"Bullshit," interrupts Nick with a smile, "we *know* we'll be seeing you."

Art laughs.

"Welfert!" bellows Aggie from the patio, "Look who's here! Bill and um..." she looks at the woman accompanying Bill "I never could remember your name," she barks, "always knew it was a funny one though!"

"Gaetane," smiles the pretty young French woman by Aggie's side.

Wilf rolls his eyes at Aggie's faux pas and goes to rescue the newly arrived guests.

∞

It's now 7:30 in the evening, and we've all eaten. Most of the kids are still outside, running off tonight's dinner, while some of the adults are outside, enjoying the early evening. Others of us have gathered in the living room. There's Wilf, Nick (whose holding Rhiann now), and Sylvie. Also Johnny, Len and Grace, and several other guests. The general conversation is around last month's federal election, and our new Prime Minister, Joe Clark. It was only a couple of weeks ago that Pierre Trudeau handed the reins of power over to Mr. Clark. It'll be interesting to see what a conservative government will bring us.

I sip my beer and sit cross-legged on the floor next to the coffee table listening to the murmur of conversation around me. Nick suddenly hands the baby over to Sylvie saying, "Oh, I think that Rhiann's had a poo."

"That's okay Rhiann," says Wilf, "I did that myself, this morning."

"Oh Welfert stop it!" bellows Aggie suddenly appearing in the doorway from the kitchen.

"Yes I did," laughs Wilf, "Why do you think I was up so early painting the front yard fence?"

"I gets up this morning and I looks out the bedroom windah," says Aggie addressing the room, "an' I started cryin' some big ol' tears and I thinks to myself, 'Jeez Welfert's so good to me. Look at him out there at 6:30 in the mornin' paintin' the fence."

"That's because I had an accidental mudslide this morning," laughs Wilf again.

Laughter rumbles through the living room.

"Bullshit! Ya did not!" barks Aggie as she thunders down the hall toward one of the bedrooms.

Wilf smiles and shrugs his shoulders and once again laughter ripples throughout the room until Aggie can be heard to shout, "My Jesus, he did too!" In an instant Aggie appears in the living room door way holding up Wilf's soiled underwear for all of us to see.

The room falls apart in laughter. I have to cover my mouth with my hand so I won't spray beer all over everybody. I can see Johnny holding his hands over his mouth while the sound of his cackling can be heard above everyone else in the room.

"Welfert! Ya shit your drawers!" she exclaims half in shock, and half mockingly.

This is the first time I've ever seen Wilf speechless and turning red. He just laughs and shrugs.

∞

I don't remember how I made it home from Wilf's party, but I vaguely recall Nick asking me if I wanted a ride. I did wake up in my bed the next morning, and I found a slip of paper with Nick and Sylvie's Calgary address and phone number in the pocket of my jeans. So I went back to Wilf's the next day to get the car.

But now it's a week later and I lie in bed staring at the ceiling. I'm thinking about that party, and I'm thinking about last night. Cheryl took me out for dinner. We went to a place that she knows in Barrie that's really "la-de-da." You know the type of place I'm talking about, white linen napkins, the best wine, fine china and silver cutlery. I felt like the old bull-in-the-china-shop, but I had some of the best prime rib that I've ever eaten. And the wine that she ordered was great, although I didn't drink very much of it because I had to drive.

Just before we left the restaurant, she handed me a small package. I opened it to find a small lapel pin with a crown at the top of it. Small, gold maple leaves border a pink coloured circle with a lone pine tree in the middle of it. The word BORDEN appears across the bottom of the circle in black and gold, and then beneath that are the words E Principio. I guess it's Latin, but I don't know what the hell it means.

"Now I'd better see that on your good suit when we see each other in Alberta," she warned as I dropped her off when the evening was through. I laughed about it as I drove home. It's funny to think that we'll only be a couple of hour's car ride from each other in Alberta.

I couldn't sleep last night, partly because I'm a little scared. I've never lived away from home before. But I also couldn't sleep because I'm excited. Calgary seems like such a long way to go to begin a new life. All night long, my mind has been racing. Thoughts about leaving home, my parents, my being so far away from them, thoughts about a new life with Bryn. What will that be like?

I fold my hands behind the back of my head as I lay staring at the ceiling once more. Even though I'm really tired, somehow I'm feeling energized.

In the light of the breaking day, I look around the room at the bare walls. All of the posters that hung on the walls, and the photos that I've shot and framed, are now safely packed away in boxes. All of my big stuff like my stereo, records, and odd bits of furniture that I've managed to collect are stored in the basement. Dad says that he'll ship everything to me when I get settled in Calgary.

I turn to look at the clock radio beside the bed, one of the few things I haven't packed away yet. I watch the digits click from 4:48 to 4:49 to 4:50. I can hear noises coming from downstairs, and my folks in the kitchen as the sounds of CBC Radio starts to mingle with their voices.

Bryn said he'd be here by seven, so I'd better be ready when he arrives. Knowing him, he'll want to pack everything in the car and get on the road PDQ.

I get out of bed, slip on a pair of jeans and a t-shirt, and make my way out of the bedroom. The sound of the gurgling coffee machine and the smell of freshly brewed coffee are growing stronger as I get closer to the kitchen. The morning sun pours through the kitchen window as I enter with a "good morning."

My parents both look at me and give me a smile. Dad sits in his usual spot at the table close to the fridge so it's within easy reach should he want anything extra to go with his meals. Mom's at the kitchen sink, and I see a gift-wrapped box on the table.

"That's for you," she smiles as she points the knife in her hand toward the box. I stand motionless looking at the unexpected prize.

Dad sips his newly poured coffee, quietly smiles at me and says, "Well don't stand there smilin' dammit, open it!"

With that, I attack the box, ripping the wrapping off it with the abandon of a child on Christmas morning. I open the lid of the unwrapped box. I bring out a red sweatshirt with some small printing on the left chest portion. It has the words *Wolloston Lake, Coe Hill, Ont.* surrounding a drawn outline of the lake. It's the place where we have a summer cottage.

I've got great memories of it, like falling out of the tree fort that Dad, me, and my brothers built. And of course the mosquitoes; the little vampires would always go for me and leave everybody else alone. Every summer long weekend and every August we would be there. But in spite of all the little things that bothered me about it, I always regretted leaving the cottage when summer was through. I haven't been back there in a couple of years, but Mom and Dad still go there faithfully every August. Frank and his girlfriend are going up there for a couple of weeks this summer.

"Where did you get this?" I ask excitedly.

Mom smiles at me then points to Dad.

I look over to Dad, and he smiles back at me. "Where do you think I went that day last week, when I was gone from the house all day long?" he says with a huge grin on his face. "Besides, if I hadn't gone, I'd still be hearing about it from your mother."

"Oh now there you go again," says Mom a little annoyed, "why do you always have to say things like that?"

"Woman, will you stop it, I was only kidding."

Just then Frank walks into the kitchen, followed closely by Pete. Pete's eyes are red like he's been rubbing them. He looks at me, then he wraps both of his arms around me, puts his head on my shoulder and keeps it there. I'm so surprised by this that I drop the shirt on the floor.

"Things aren't gonna be the same anymore," he whimpers.

This isn't like Pete at all. He lifts his head and silently looks at me with his reddened eyes. Then he tightens his hold on me once more, closes his eyes, and rests his head on my shoulder again.

Mom, Dad and Frank look at the two of us and smile. I'm at a loss for what to do. Pete has never displayed this kind of emotion toward me before. My first reaction is to push him away from me, but I put one of my hands on top of his head. I look at my father for some kind of sign as to what to do next. Dad smiles at me and nods his head, so I rest my head on top of Pete's.

"I wanna go to Calgary with you and Bryn," he says in a whimper.

"You can always come out for visits, Pete," I say him, "and who knows, maybe when you finish school you can move out there with me if you want."

"I don't wanna stay in Angus." Pete pouts like a young child, his head still on my shoulder.

I look over to Dad and Frank. Frank rolls his eyes while Dad chuckles at the sight of us.

"Will you two give it a rest," says Dad still chuckling.

"Yeah, you're breakin' my heart here," says Frank.

The three of them are smiling, and I really feel embarrassed because I don't know how to handle this.

I pick up the shirt and put it on the back of my chair, gently breaking Pete's hold on me.

Frank says, "Pete we're all gonna miss him, so can the drama!"

Like a small child, Pete is further upset by Frank's remark and retreats to his room.

Dad heaves an exasperated sigh, "For Chrissakes Frank, why did you upset him?"

"I didn't mean to, Dad."

"Go apologize," says Mom.

"But Mom—"

"Go apologize, now!" Dad says.

"Oh Jeez," Frank says with a deep sigh. Rolling his eyes, he leaves the kitchen and goes down the hall to Pete's room. "Hey Pete, I'm sorry, I didn't mean that."

I silently pour myself a cup of coffee and sit at the table.

"I didn't think that my leaving home would be so heavy. I kind of feel bad."

"Now that's bullshit, Son," says Dad as he takes another sip of coffee.

"Maybe you're feeling a touch guilty about Pete's reaction. You need to get out and make a life of your own. Don't feel bad about that."

"I guess you're right."

"Like Frank says, we're all sad to see you go, but Pete will get over it," says Mom.

I sip my coffee, and the conversation revolves around future plans about Calgary as Pete and Frank reappear. Frank grabs a coffee from the pot, and Pete sits beside me at the table with a bit of a smile on his face.

"Feelin' better, Son?" Dad asks him as he rubs the top of Pete's head.

Pete smiles quietly and shrugs his shoulders.

"He's fine," says Frank. "He'll feel a lot better once he gets some breakfast in him."

We have breakfast together. In the next couple of hours I have a shower, get dressed, pack my remaining items away, and make some last minute checks to see that I've remembered to bring everything that I'll need. I move all of my gear from my bedroom to the front door, then we're all back in the kitchen sitting around the table talking.

"So you're all going to come out for the stampede next year, right?" I say to everyone as if we've rehearsed what the answer will be.

"We'll see what happens, Son," Dad says with a grin.

I'm about to make a smart-assed remark back at him when a knock comes to the door. I glance at my watch, and it's quarter to seven. I go to the front door, and there's Bryn with that smirk on his face that he gets when it looks like he's ready to burst at the seams. I open the door and greet him.

"Ready to go?" asks Bryn excitedly.

Greetings with Bryn are exchanged as the family joins us at the door.

"I'll help you put things in the car," says Bryn as we gather my bags and take them down to Le Car. As we're beginning to load my bags, Bryn says to me, "Why don't you say goodbye to your folks, and I'll pack things in here."

I look to my parents standing on the doorstep watching us. I go back to them, and Mom kisses me and gives me a hug, "Now you call us as soon as you get to Calgary."

"I will, Mom," I promise like an elementary school kid.

Dad and I go to shake hands, but we embrace instead. My eyes are closed as he says, "Take care of yourself, Son."

I remain in the same position. "I will, Dad. You too."

"We will."

Frank and I hug each other. "Even though you didn't get a straight answer this morning, *I'll* be coming out to visit you for Stampede next year," he says with a grin.

"Give me lots of notice so I can make myself scarce," I answer.

"I'll be seeing you soon, so have the beer cold," Frank says.

Then I turn expecting to see Pete, but he's not around.

"Where's Pete?" I ask.

"He's gone to his room," says Dad. "I don't think he's over the emotional state he's in."

"I never thought that he would take this so badly," I say bewildered.

"Well," says Dad, "if you were moving to Toronto, I don't think he'd be reacting this way. But since you're moving a couple of thousand miles away…"

"I see what you mean."

"I wish I had a camera this morning," laughs Frank. "You should have seen the look on your face when Pete hugged you."

Dad laughs, "Yeah, talk about the deer in the headlights."

I laugh, picturing how I might have looked.

"Anyway," Dad continues, "I think you'll find that Pete's as surprised by his show of emotion this morning as you were. He may be feeling a bit embarrassed by it as well."

"Maybe I should go say goodbye to him?"

"No, I think Pete just wants to be alone for a bit."

I look for a moment in the direction of Pete's room.

"Send him a postcard while you're on the road," Mom says. "Maybe when you get to Calgary give him a phone call."

I smile. "Good idea," I say, "that's exactly what I'll do."

Bryn, who has just finished packing the car, joins us. He shakes hands with Dad and Frank, and gives Mom a big hug.

"Now Bryn, look after my baby boy," says Mom with a smile and a wink to Bryn.

"Mom," I say with a growl in my voice. I hate it when she does that, even if she is only kidding.

Bryn laughs, then looks at me and says, "I'll look after your baby boy."

"Thanks a hell of a lot," I say to him.

Then he laughs again.

"And make sure you drop us a card while you're on the road," Dad says.

"Okay, I will," I promise.

Bryn and I head back to Le Car. I turn back and wave a final time to everybody. I get into Bryn's car and roll down the window. We all wave as Bryn starts the car. We pull away from the curb and drive down the street. Bryn waves a goodbye to everyone as we pull out.

"You okay?" Bryn asks.

"Yeah, although Pete's not taking my going away very well." I tell Bryn about Pete's emotional display this morning before breakfast.

Bryn smirks, "He'll get over it."

"Yeah, I guess so."

I watch the passing scenery as we leave Angus and drive along Highway 90 to Barrie. I think of the many times that I've driven along this stretch of road during the last few years. It seems very different today; this morning as I sit in the passenger seat and watch the world go by, all of these things seem strangely new. It's almost like I've never seen them before.

We approach the small hamlet of Utopia. Utopia is actually off of the highway a little way, but all you can see from the road is a blue and white, fifties-style trailer home with the town's name on a lonely little sign across the road from it. I chuckle as the irony of the scene dawns on me for the first time ever. I wonder when I'll be seeing all of this again.

Bryn's eyes are fixed on the road. There is a quiet tone to his voice. "We'll be on the open highway soon."

I'm so lost in thought that, before I know it, Bryn's taking a turn onto Highway 11 outside of Barrie north to Orillia. Bryn switches on the tape player and turns it loud. As in most cases when Bryn turns on his tape machine, he sings along with the song. I join in the chorus of *Deacon Blues* by Steely Dan as we drive out of Barrie. A new page in my book of life is about to be written.

∞

We've put on a lot of miles this morning. We came through Orillia, and north through cottage country— little places with names like Bracebridge and Huntsville surrounded by hundreds of miles of forest, lots of lakes, lots of camping and fishing, and lots of tourists!

Right now we're about 20 clicks north of North Bay. We stopped briefly in town to pick up a few supplies at a supermarket, and a quick look at my watch tells me it's time for lunch. We drive into a roadside picnic ground by the mouth of a river as it flows into a lake. We find one of the few vacant picnic tables left and quickly claim it for an hour or so. Bryn gets the cooler from the back of the car and I get some sandwich fixings out. We throw together some sandwiches, crack open a beer each, and then eat. A strong breeze blows, and it's a welcomed relief from this hot June day.

Afterward we go for a short walk. The breeze continues to blow through the trees, creating a noisy rustle above our heads. It's early afternoon, and the only other sound we hear is the water as it flows into the nearby lake. We walk in silence. I wish I had the balls to hold his hand while we walk, but I don't. The thought of other people staring at us embarrasses me as I know it would Bryn.

Just then the roar of a transport truck thunders down the highway outside the grounds. Like an unwanted party guest, it belches and farts as it rumbles by. Its clamouring, thumping, and farting reaches a crescendo then starts to fade. It continues down the highway, its cacophony steadily fading until the voices of the river and the wind through the trees are the only sounds we hear once more. Bryn looks at his watch. We agree that it's time to get back on the road if we're going to make Kapuskasing by early evening.

I'm now in the driver's seat for the next few hours as the Trans-Canada Highway rolls ahead of us north to Cochrane then makes a sharp left turn northwest to Kapuskasing. Bryn watches the passing scenery in silence, and I tap my hands on the steering wheel in time to a song on my Max Webster tape.

Bryn turns to me and says with a smile and a nudge to my side, "Will you stop drumming your hands like that, it's driving me crazy."

"Oh, okay," I answer, surprised and my hands come to an abrupt stop.

It's late afternoon as we arrive at a small town called Moonbeam. This is the place on the highway where I make a right turn north onto Highway 581.

It's a secondary highway that travels almost in a straight line from Moonbeam to Remi Lake. Rene Brunelle Provincial Park is just northwest of us, but we've found a great little campground here on the south end of the lake. We find a spot and I can see a couple of seaplanes floating idly by a dock across a cove from where we're camping.

Bryn stops the car and gets out, I follow suit, but fuck, the blackflies! Millions of them! I'm being eaten alive by the fucking blackflies! A huge cloud of them swarms above me, landing on every bit of my exposed flesh they can. This causes me to perform quite a dance as I jerk my head from side-to-side while waving my arms around to keep them away, and hitting various parts of my body as they land. Bryn almost splits a gut as he laughs at my madman's dance.

I jump back in the car, fumble through my bag, and bring out a bottle of insect repellent. Dad warned me that I would need it, and he was right. I smear it over my face, neck, arms and legs then throw a hat on. I get back out of the car and even though the blackflies are no longer biting me, they still hover in clouds over my head. No matter where I go, when I look behind me, there they are.

I notice a spot on the side of Bryn's neck where blood is trickling down from a small wound. It looks like he's been bitten by a blackfly and isn't aware of it. Once more, he doesn't seem to be bothered by them. He very calmly puts on insect repellant anyway, and we pitch Bryn's tent within short walking distance of a small, white building with a sign that says "comfort station." It's obviously where the washrooms and public showers are.

As soon as the tent is set up, Bryn disappears inside, zipping up the flap. When he emerges, only a few minutes later, he's dressed in his running clothes. He puts bug repellent on his now-exposed flesh and says, "I'll be gone for about an hour."

"In that case I'll have a nap while you're gone. I'm tired after driving and not sleeping very well last night."

I watch him for a few minutes as he does some stretching exercises and then he runs down the gravel road disappearing around a bend, a cloud of blackflies in hot pursuit. I crawl into the tent, quickly closing the flap and strip down to my underwear then crawl into my sleeping bag and close my eyes.

In what seems an instant, I'm awakened by Bryn unzipping the front opening of the tent, and crawling in having finished his run.

"Sorry, Neil," puffs Bryn, sweat pouring down his face.

"You finished your run already?" I ask in a still-bleary state.

"Yeah," he says as he quickly climbs into the tent, "It's been just about an hour. I'm gonna have a shower," he says as he hurriedly zips up the flap plunging us both into the dim light and safety of the tent.

"Hope that you left the blackflies outside," I say.

He laughs as he searches around the tent for a towel and his shaving gear then he says, "Okay I'm going for a shower. I'll be back in a bit." And with that he exits the tent.

∞

Except for the faint light at the comfort station entrance, it's dark in the tent. Cool night air circulates through the small opened top flaps on both ends of the tent. I watch a cluster of mosquitoes in the dim light as they hover at the open tent flap; only the insect netting that spans the openings keeps them away from us.

The campground is silent for the most part, except for the distant murmur of a handful of campers on the other side of the grounds who are still talking around their fires. At least they've got their music turned down. But it's the sound from within this tent that I'm listening to. I hear the rhythmic breathing of Bryn as he sleeps. I want to hold him close to me. I want to touch him, but instead I slip back down into the sleeping bag and go back to sleep.

∞

The eardrum-shattering roar of a seaplane taking off from across the cove startles me awake. Shit, I just about jump through the top of the tent! Daylight has illuminated the campground, and I wonder what the fuck time it is. I try to focus my eyes on my watch. It's 6 am!

"Thanks asshole," I say as I pull one of my pillows over my head to try to muffle the sound. The earsplitting roar assaults us, as the whole campsite jumps from the comfort of warm sleeping bags at the sound of this heart-stopping reveille.

The plane is airborne. It doesn't care at all for those of us that are still reeling from this assault. It just sails into the sky leaving a dazed and cursing campground behind it.

As we all reluctantly come to life, I turn to look at the mass of sleeping bag beside me. Somewhere under there is Bryn. I hear him moan something about getting his hands on the son-of-a-bitch responsible for this. I rub what I guess to be his shoulder, get dressed, splash my exposed skin with insect repellant and go outside to light the camp stove for coffee. Bryn follows me out of the tent about twenty minutes later with his shaving gear and towel in hand.

"G'mornin," I say.

He looks at me and gives me a big warm smile. "It is a good morning except for that asshole plane." Then he disappears into the campground washroom facilities.

I have the first sip of my coffee and survey the campground by early morning light. The tents that surround us stir with activity, and one-by-one people emerge, bleary-eyed, and start up their Coleman stoves. I watch the crows as they bitch at each other over who claims a prized leftover morsel of food two campsites away. One picks it up while the others try to coax it from him. Back and forth they play tug-of-war with it until one of them takes flight with it in its mouth. The others take off after him squawking at him to drop it.

Half an hour has passed, and Bryn returns freshly showered. He's smiling and has a spring in his step as he approaches our campsite.

He puts his shower gear down on the seat of the picnic table, "I'm ready for that coffee, Mr. DeMille," he says as he gives his hands a clap and rubs them together. He pours himself a cup and sits at the table across from me.

"So Calgary," he smiles, "we're well on our way."

"Here, here," I say as we clack our melmac mugs together. "I've been wondering what it will be like to live there. I mean, I don't imagine Calgary would be like Toronto."

"You've got that right," Bryn says and takes a hasty gulp of coffee. "Hey look, I want you to do me a favour while I'm driving today."

"What's that?"

He goes to the car and rummages through his backpack in the trunk. He comes back to the table and throws a copy of Kurt Vonnegut's *Slaughterhouse Five* in front of me.

"Let's read this to each other while we're driving today just to pass the miles by."

I pick the book up and run my thumb over the pages, fanning them.

"I've been wanting to read it for years," Bryn continues, "but I somehow have never seemed to find the time to do it. I figure this way we both could enjoy it."

"Sounds good to me," I say, "but I have to warn you, I'm not much into reading. So my voice could sound a little rough"

"That's okay."

"Oh by the way," I say suddenly remembering something that I wanted to show Bryn, "I brought something along that my mother photocopied for us."

"What is it?"

I go to the car and go through my things. I bring the stapled photocopies back and put them on the table in front of Bryn. "Mom gets Chatelaine Magazine and this was in the latest issue. She thought that we might find it useful."

It's an eight-page feature on Calgary, the people, the places to hang out, the city's attitude, the main political players, the business climate, etc. While Bryn is paging through the article, I produce something else to show him, the latest edition of The Body Politic.

He looks a little taken aback when he realizes what I've brought out. His eyes dart around at the surrounding campsites with an obvious nervousness. "What are you doing with that?" he demands in a low voice.

"Relax Bryn," I say calmly, "people can't see what this is unless they come up to the table and sit down with us."

I see his body relax a bit, but he still eyes The Body Politic like Anita Bryant herself is going to leap out of the magazine onto the table top and scream "FAGGOT!" at him.

"I brought this along," I continue in a low voice, "because it has the listings of some organizations that I thought we should check out when we get to Calgary."

Bryn says nothing.

"If this is scarin' you, I'll put it away and we can have a look at it when nobody else is around, okay?"

He silently nods in agreement as I put it back in the car, out of sight.

We finish our coffee, have breakfast, take down the tent, pack everything away, and within a couple of hours we're ready to get back to the road, Bryn taking his place in the driver's seat with me riding shotgun. Bryn turns and looks at me.

"Look Neil, I guess I was kind of out of line when you brought The Body Politic out, and I'm sorry about that. I'm still not used to this. I hope that you can understand that."

"I wouldn't have brought it out if I didn't think it would be safe to do so."

"Sorry," Bryn says sheepishly.

"No prob, bub. And hey, I do understand where you're coming from."

"Well, thanks, I appreciate that. We'll have a look at those listings as we get closer to Calgary."

"Well Captain," I say, "If we are to reach the wild planet of hot cowboys then I suggest we get going."

"Eee-haw, Mr. Spock," Bryn says and gives a thumbs up.

"Most illogical Captain."

Bryn laughs, puts the car in gear, and we leave the campsite. As we pull out onto the road that leads to the Trans-Canada Highway, Bryn puts his hand on my knee, rubs the length of it, looks at me, smiles and winks. I laugh and squeeze my hand around his. He keeps smiling and turns his attention back to the road.

"I put that book in the glove compartment," he says.

I open the glove compartment and pull out Slaughterhouse Five. "Do you want me to start reading it now?" I ask.

"Why not?"

I open the cover and begin to read chapter one, *"Billy Pilgrim became unstuck in time..."* For the next twenty minutes I stumble my way through the novel, and eventually we stop for gas at a small town called Hearst. I can't believe this, everything here is in French! All of my life I've lived in this province, and I never knew that French was the first language up in these parts. The signs are all French, and when we stop at a gas station, the handsome little guy with the dark moustache running the gas pump greets us in French. Luckily Bryn is fluent in the language and he carries on a conversation with the guy as if we were in the middle of Québec.

He gets out of the car and the two of them stand beside the vehicle as they talk. I don't understand what they're talking about, so I silently continue to read the book wishing that I had paid more attention to French class in high school.

Bryn pays the guy and gets back in the car.

"He's kinda cute," I observe.

Bryn smiles, "As far as I'm concerned, most French guys are."

With that, he turns the ignition and we're headed west to the towns of Longlac, then on to Geraldton.

∞

I read to Bryn while we're driving along the highway, and I stop every once in a while and look out at the changing scenery as we go. I've noticed that, since we've entered Longlac, the landscape has changed quite a bit. The land around Kapuskasing and Hearst was rolling, and I can see how it's become quite different. In fact, from Longlac through to Geraldton, the terrain is pretty flat. Although it can be hard to tell because miles of trees line both sides of the highway.

It's like we're in an entirely new world with new features and new inhabitants all passing by outside of these car windows.

"I wouldn't mind stopping to stretch my legs," Bryn says.

"Yeah, I could go for something cold to drink as well," I agree.

"Are there any picnic areas close by?"

"I'll have a look," I say taking the road map from the glove compartment.

I study the map carefully. "Captain," I say, "there appears to be a small planet ahead called MacDiarmid. There also appears to be a picnic area nearby."

"Prepare to beam down soon, Mr Spock," says Bryn.

"Aye aye, Captain," I say, snapping a crisp salute.

∞

Bryn and I sit at the picnic table, drinking the apple juice that we bought from a gas station nearby. I'm watching him as he scribbles a list of supplies that we should get once we hit Thunder Bay.

"Hey Bryn, I want to show you something."

"What's that?"

"Just wait a sec," I say as I go to the car and search through one of my bags. Ah, there they are. I take out the copy of The Body Politic that I brought out earlier, and slip them inside. I take the paper to Bryn and put it in front of him. He stares at the paper for a few seconds and looks at me.

He shrugs his shoulders and says, "You showed me this earlier."

"Open it," I prod. As Bryn opens the paper his eyes grow wide and his mouth drops open. They're the naked photos that Jeff took of me during that weekend in Toronto back in March. Bryn just stares at them like he's never seen a naked guy before. He looks back at me, smiles, and says nothing.

"I figure since nobody's around it's safe to show you them."

He looks back to the photos. He smirks, "Can I have one of these?"

"Why do you think that I brought them out in the first place?"Bryn stuffs one of the Polaroids back inside the paper, goes to the car, and puts it in a side pocket of his weekend bag *for safekeeping* he says.

We pack everything up in the back of the car. I get in the car, but Bryn has to take a leak before we go. Within a few minutes he's back. Bryn gets in the car and says, "Here hang on to this." He hands me the shopping list that he's been busy scribbling, so I stuff it in my pocket and we do up our seat belts and continue on our way.

We fly south on Highway 17, entering the Thunder Bay city limits in what seems like hardly anytime at all. At that point the highway rounds a bend, and we're driving along the edge of a scenic escarpment with the city of Thunder Bay hugging the northwestern shore of Lake Superior before us. I notice a sign indicating a look out point coming up to our right.

"Pull over here," I say to Bryn. "I want to have a look at the city."

Bryn obliges me and we pull over. Taking my camera with me, I get out of the car and walk to the edge of the lookout point. Bryn stands beside me as we stare at the city opening her arms to us. The city hugs the shoreline as far as we can see while the sun shines on her downtown section, casting an eerie glow as a wall of dark grey approaches from Lake Superior. I can see the outline of the Sleeping Giant silhouetted against this darkened backdrop. Ancient Indian legend has it that the rock formation that forms the Sleeping Giant was once a real giant. As I look at it, it kind of looks like a giant profile of a human face protruding up from the lake.

The two of us look out over this small but bustling city. I snap a few pictures as the wind begins to blow stronger and dark clouds slowly move on shore from Lake Superior.

"Maybe it's time that we looked for a supermarket or something," says Bryn. "It looks like it's going to rain."

I agree, so the two of us get into the car and head into the city. We follow the main road until we're driving in the west side of Thunder Bay. What a busy little place! Everywhere I look people and vehicles are scurrying back and forth at a dizzying pace.

Bryn hangs a right, and luckily we're near a shopping mall on the way to Kakabeka Falls Provincial Park. We turn into a swirl of mid afternoon activity in the shopping mall parking lot. We dodge the chaos of shoppers frantically trying to get to wherever-it-is they're going. Some, like us, are heading into the mall, while others, shopping carts loaded with screaming kids in tow, are trying to leave with everything intact.

We walk past an overweight woman in cut-offs, a striped halter top, and blue rubber flip-flops. She jostles with three bags of groceries and two screeching, crying kids, struggling to get all of them safely inside the car. The woman puts the groceries in the back seat of the car and, brandishing a lit cigarette between two fingers, she waves them firmly at the car while shouting, "Get into de goddamn car 'fore I crown yuz!" The kids shut up and crawl inside the vehicle, sniffling as they go.

The men, for the most part, sport trucker's caps, plaid jackets, cases of beer, and foul mouths, just like the old road gang that I worked with—Art, Nick, Johnny and Wilf, man, I miss them. Life is weird, and it'll be weird when I get to Calgary and see Nick and his family there. Jeez, I guess it really brings that old saying *life goes on* into reality. Another city, 2,000 miles away from home, and Nick and his family will be living there with me. And of course Art said that he and Johnny would be out to The Stampede this summer with the horses. I shake my head in wonder at where time brings everybody.

"Did you bring the small list that I made when we stopped at planet Macdiarmid?" Bryn asks.

"Aye aye, Captain," I answer like Mr. Spock and fumble through both of my pants pockets, forgetting which one I put it in. I remove the rumpled piece of paper containing the list out of my right pocket and give it to him.

We walk into the supermarket. All I can hear is the passing snatches of conversation from the crowd-weary shoppers:

—How much is the relish?

—I want Fruit Loops! I want Fruit Loops!

—I didn't want to bring you in the first place!

—Jason get back here!

—T'hell with this metric system!

We manage to survive the ravages of the suburban mall crowd and get back to Le Car in one piece. I didn't even notice what the total of the food bill was. I try to give Bryn some money for it, and he says that's okay, maybe I can get the next one. I shrug my shoulders and put the money back in my pocket. Bryn opens the trunk of the car and takes out the cooler. He fills it with the things we just got then we rearrange the back of the car. Ah shit; I forgot to get a post card for Pete like I told my family I would yesterday. Well, maybe when we hit Winnipeg, I'll send him one from there.

We are back on the Trans-Canada Highway heading west out of Thunder Bay on the short stretch of road to the town of Kakabeka Falls. I'm at the wheel again with Bryn riding shotgun.

"Captain," I say, "why do you want to visit this Kakabeka Falls?"

"Well, Mr. Spock," says Bryn, "I understand it's beautiful, and I've wanted to see it for a while."

"And the inhabitants, Captain, what are they like?"

"The inhabitants are humanoid—"

"More's the pity."

"Ah yes," he says, "anyway, I'd like to remain here overnight if you're not in a hurry to get to the Winnipeg Quadrant, Mr. Spock.

"Captain, I'm sure the crew wouldn't mind an overnight stay here."

"I knew you'd see it my way, Mr. Spock."

I shake my head like Mr. Spock would and mutter, "Fascinating."

We laugh and, before we know it, we're turning off of the main highway into Kakabeka Falls Provincial Park. We find a campsite in the smaller of the two camping areas and set up the tent. As we're finishing I rub my hand on the side of my neck, only to draw it back and see blood on my fingers. "Hmmm," I say.

"What?" asks Bryn.

"I guess I was bitten by a blackfly," I say holding my fingers to show him, "and I didn't even know it."

"Gettin' used to it, huh," he says as he winks at me.

"I guess so," I say with a shrug.

"Hey, wanna go for a walk before dinner?"

"Yeah, it'd be nice to stretch my legs a bit."

So with that, we finish with the tent, secure the car, then we set off toward the sound of the falls.

As we walk along one of the many trails, I can't help but be taken in by the beauty of this place. A swift roaring river runs nearby, while a light mist shrouds the trail we walk on, and as we get closer to the falls, a cool breeze puts its arms around me.

We don't have to walk much further and there they are: the falls themselves. They drop 39 meters over a sheer cliff, creating a turbulent and frothy eddy at its base.

Bryn takes some photos of it, and then we move further along the trail for a closer look. What I wouldn't give for a joint to smoke about now. We come to a full stop at a point in the trail where we're on an observation platform looking onto the top of the falls. The roar is deafening, and our skin glistens as mist settles everywhere.

"This is great!" I yell to Bryn trying to be heard above the roar. He looks at me and gives me that crooked smile of his again. Bryn takes a few more pictures. "I'm gettin' a bit hungry!" he yells.

"Yeah! Let's go back for supper!"

∞

We've eaten dinner a few hours ago, and now we're sitting in front of a blazing campfire. We've been hearing the rumble of thunder in the distance, and little-by-little the rumblings have become louder. But we don't move from our places by the fire.

"I admire you, Neil," Bryn says in a mournful tone. "You've done things with your life that I've only dreamed about."

"I find that hard to believe Bryn. You've been to New York City, you've got a college education and the promise of a career for the next five years."

"You don't understand. You're free."

I'm puzzled. "I still don't know what you mean, Bryn."

He sighs. "You can be yourself Neil. I can't."

"Of course, you can."

Bryn shakes his head, "I have too much at stake. The military doesn't take kindly to gay guys being in their ranks. I could get a dishonourable discharge just for having the feelings that I do. And I'm not sure how my sisters would react if they knew that I have homosexual feelings."

"Do you think they would freak out? "

"I know it's a real possibility."

We're silent. Meanwhile another clap of thunder rumbles, sounding a lot closer to us.

Bryn smiles. "I think that storm that was approaching Thunder Bay has followed us here," he says.

"Yeah, I think you're right."

Just then a flash of lightening brightens the sky overhead, and an earsplitting clap of thunder seems to shake the very ground we're on. We both look at each other and say, "Uh oh."

No sooner do the words escape our mouths than the rain pisses down on us. Like two proverbial chickens with our heads cut off, we scurry around the campsite, closing and locking the car, shutting and locking the Coleman stove, trying to put as many things as possible on the table so we can cover them with the tarp that just happens to be laying beside the tent.

As I scurry, I catch a glimpse of surrounding campsites and see them doing the same as us. The whole scene strikes me as funny, and I laugh. Bryn laughs as well. What a sight all of us must be, running around in the pouring rain, getting soaked in the process trying to secure everything that can possibly blow away in the storm.

Everything secured, we both crawl into the tent, still laughing like idiots. Dripping wet, we both stretch back on the sleeping bags and laugh. As our laughter subsides, we find ourselves looking into each others' eyes. I'm feeling a strong rush of desire like I've never felt before.

Bryn breaks the spell. "I've gotta get out of these wet clothes," he says. He rummages around for something and finally says, "Ah here it is." The brightness of his flashlight makes everything clearer.

"Now I know I've got some dry clothes in here," he continues searching through the weekend bag by his side. He peels off his wet t-shirt and then continues to look through the bag.

I watch him as he undresses, and each bit of clothing that comes off his body makes me harder. I want to reach out and touch him. Much to my surprise, I do.

I reach over and put my hand gently in the middle of his back. His body stiffens and he sits motionless. Even though I'm a little nervous about his reaction, I keep my hand right where it is. He does nothing. So I run my hand up his back to his shoulder and begin to gently massage it like I did that night in his room. He still doesn't resist.

I sit up and gently put my other hand on his other shoulder and begin to massage it. His head slowly falls forward as I move my hands to the base of his neck and knead his flesh. I'm pushed on by the desire that's built in me as I bring my face close to his flesh and gently lick the nape of his neck. I feel my cock getting harder and harder. I run my tongue along the back of his neck again. I quickly take off my shirt and help him out of his wet pants.

Bryn leans his now naked body against me. I continue to massage his shoulders, and I kiss his neck again. I rub my swollen crotch against his back, and he turns his face to mine. Our faces are so close to each other that I can feel his breath mingle with mine. Our lips meet. We kiss as I slowly move my hands from his shoulders to his chest where I gently play with his nipples. A moan escapes his throat. Then I slowly move my hand down to his cock. I can feel it swelling in my hand as I gently squeeze it. He puts his hand on my swollen crotch, which is now aching to be free from the confines of my pants. Then he turns to me and we kiss again.

I sit back, take off my shoes and socks, and slide my pants off. Here we are, both of us naked. We say nothing we just look in each other's eyes.

I smile and bring his face to meet mine. We kiss again, deeply. I put my arms around him as I lay Bryn back onto the sleeping bags. I grab the flashlight and extinguish the brightness. I become more aggressive as I crawl on top of him. We hold each other closely in the darkness, our mouths touch and our pent up passion overtakes us. Bryn passively lets me take him as the rain pelts against the tent, and the thunder loudly rolls as if to cheer me on.

∞

I lay in the darkness of the night. The rain stopped about twenty minutes ago but I can still hear the roar of the falls not too far away. The smell of sex still permeates the tent. The salt from his sweat still covers my body and his smell still lingers in my moustache. A smile comes across my mouth.

I decide to survey the damage outside. I get up and unzip the tent flap just enough to stick my head outside to have a look. I slowly look around. The clouds have parted and only the moon lights the campsite. Water gently drips off the branches of the surrounding trees like tears and our campfire is nothing more than a smouldering wet pile of blackened wood.

But the air is fresh, and I feel like I'm looking at the world with a new pair of eyes for some reason. I take a satisfied deep breath, zip the tent flap up and go to sleep.

∞

Daylight. It feels cool this morning, but the first rays of sunlight are peeking through the shadows of the trees on to the tent. I turn and look at the mass of sleeping bag beside me. Once again, somewhere under there is Bryn. I rub his shoulder; at least I think it's his shoulder. Bryn rolls over and looks at me. He says nothing but the look on his face has me transfixed. He has that big shit-eating grin on his face again and he won't take his eyes from me.

"Neil…"

"Yeah?"

"I think I love you."

We stare into each other's eyes, wearing the stupidest smiles I'm sure anybody has seen. Then as if on cue the both of us break into laughter, then try to shush each other so as to not to wake the whole campsite.

He pulls me to him and we kiss like we've never kissed before. I feel as if my body is penetrating the very core of who he is. We're locked on each other's mouths.

∞

It's almost an hour later, and we're lying in each others arms. The world has now sprung to life all around us while we lay in silence.

"I guess I should get up and start the stove."

"Hmmmphh," grunts Bryn sleepily.

I laugh, get dressed, splash insect repellant all over, and go outside.

∞

As we finish breakfast Bryn says, "Oh, I almost forgot. I told my sister that I would call her while I was on the road. Before we get on the road this morning I want to give her a call."

"Why don't you make the call now. I can clean this up."

He agrees and goes into the tent to get his wallet. Then he comes back out, smiles and winks at me, then goes off to the campground office to find a telephone.

∞

It's been over an hour since Bryn went to make his phone call. I'm really concerned as to what's going on. If he couldn't find a phone, I would think he'd have come back here and he could make the phone call from elsewhere—unless, of course, he's having one hell of a conversation with them.

Since he's been making his call, I've busied myself cleaning up and packing away our entire campsite. The breakfast mess is cleaned up, the sleeping bags and air mattresses are packed, the tent has been cleaned out and packed in the car, along with the cooler. I've packed everything into Le Car, and now I sit here reading Slaughterhouse Five and wondering what's happened to him.

Just as I decide to go and search for him, I see him walking down the road toward campsite.

"Hey!" I yell to him, "Did you have to walk back to Thunder Bay to use the phone?"

He doesn't answer. As he gets closer I notice there's a strange look on his face.

This concerns me. "Bryn what's the matter? Has something happened?"

He still says nothing, in fact he walks right by like I'm not there. He looks around the campsite.

"Oh," he says distractedly, "you've packed everything up."

"Yeah, it gave me something to do while I was waiting for you. Did you phone your sisters?"

"Um yeah," Bryn's body noticeably tenses. He's fidgeting like he doesn't know what to do next.

"Has something happened Bryn? Are your sisters okay?"

"Yeah," he says nervously.

"And are you okay?"

"Yeah."

Silence.

"Ummm, look, uuhh," Bryn seems like he's searching for something to say. "Let's say we get on the road since you've got everything packed away." Then he gives me a forced smirk.

"Okay," I answer. I don't like this sudden mood shift with Bryn.

"I'll drive," he says.

I ride shotgun again. Almost immediately upon entering Le Car I notice something is very different. I can feel a wall between us like I've never felt before. Bryn starts the car, grabs the first music tape that he can find, and puts it on. Jeff Beck starts playing his guitar and Bryn takes the unusual step of turning the music up to almost full volume. We drive out of the park.

I turn the volume down to a more reasonable level.

"Bryn talk to me. What's happened?"

"Nothin'."

"This is the biggest nothin' I've ever felt."

Silence.

"Is your family okay?"

"I told you they're okay," he snaps.

"C'mon Bryn this is me you're talking to."

"I told you, nothin's the matter."

"Well fine. You'll eventually tell me," I say as I sit back and gaze at the passing scenery. I glance back to Bryn every once in a while. What's happened? Why won't he tell me what's wrong? I find myself stroking the right side of my moustache once more as I'm thinking how strange this is. His mood has changed so dramatically and so quickly. Is it me? Why is he suddenly behaving like I'm somebody to be nervous of?

I put my hand on his knee like I've done before. His body stiffens and he moves my hand away from him. I don't like this. So I decide that maybe it's time to force Bryn to say something about what's going on.

"Have I done something to piss you off, Bryn?"

Silence.

"If I have, you should let me know what it is."

More silence, and I can feel that wall between us grow stronger.

"Dammit Bryn, talk to me! Something's been bugging your ass ever since you got back from phoning your sisters. Don't tell me that nothin's wrong 'cause that's bullshit. Now what the hell's eatin' you?"

Bryn stares straight ahead as he drives. His face is rigid; his body stiffens as he straightens his back. He won't look at me.

"I'm waiting Bryn, and I'm not going to stop until you tell me what the hell is going on here."

His mouth slackens a bit, and he takes a deep breath like he has some dark secret he's about to tell.

"Neil, I've been doing some thinking," he says. "It was a mistake for me to ask you along on this trip."

"What?"

"You shouldn't have come with me on this trip."

"Are you serious, Bryn?"

There's a tremble in Bryn's voice, as he speaks, "About last night," he clears his throat, and then continues, "Look, Neil, I'm not gay"

"You're not."

"No."

"Then what the hell were you last night? Or even this morning?"

"I'm serious, Neil."

"So am I. And just what the hell have you been all of these months then?"

"Look Neil, I should have just let you move to Toronto like you wanted to do in the first place. I think that you have a problem."

"I have a problem? Tell me what my problem is."

"It seems to me that you like to chase straight guys."

I break into hysterical laughter. "This is a joke, right? I like chasing straight guys?" I laugh again. "I like to chase straight guys. That's funny."

Bryn sounds like he's looking for the right words to say, "I'm not gay."

"Okay, so you're bi. I can live with that."

"Look this whole trip together was a big mistake."

"Wait a minute here. Are you saying that you haven't encouraged me at all? Are you telling me that you haven't had feelings for me all these months? Are you telling me that I've forced myself on you all along?"

"No, no look, Neil, I know that I may have, well, led you on a bit—"

"Who was it that told me he thought he was in love me this morning?"

Bryn's derailed and he seems to be consciously trying to stick to his train of thought. "And I'm sorry about that. I said that in the spur of the moment. But you're imagining things if you think that any serious kind of relationship can happen between us. I'm straight."

I don't know whether to laugh out loud or cuff him across the head.

"How about the night we kissed in your room? Was I imagining things then? How straight were you then? Or how about last night? Was I imagining things then?"

"Neil. Sometimes in a given situation," Bryn lectures paternalistically, "guys will play together. That's just the way it is. It's nothing serious, and it bothers me that you're reading more into this than what's there."

I grab the map from the dashboard, roll it into a cone, I put it to my mouth and point it at him, "Earth to Bryn! Earth to Bryn! Where the fuck have you been the last couple of months?"

"What are you talking about?"

"Will you listen to yourself? You sound like an idiot! Wasn't it you who asked me to come out west to be with you? Now you're giving me this bullshit line that this was all a mistake and you're straight?"

"Look Neil, sometimes things just happen. You're going to have to accept that. You've been kidding yourself if you think that you can get a straight guy—"

"Fuck off with the straight guy bullshit will ya? Who's kidding who? It's not *me* who's kidding myself."

"Look, I'll drop you off at your friends' place in Winnipeg, and I'm going to Calgary alone."

"You're going to Calgary alone," I repeat.

"I think that it's better that way for both of us, okay?"

I silently look at him. This kind of shit is really bugging me.

"Look," says Bryn, "I told my sisters and brothers-in-law about you being gay and they didn't think that it was a good idea for you to come along with me."

"You didn't tell them that you're gay?"

Bryn turns quickly and looks at me. For the first time since I've known him I can see deep terror in his eyes.

"Aha! So you *are* afraid of what they're going to think about you being gay. That's what's eatin' you, isn't it?"

"That's not it."

"Tell me what is it then."

He's silent for a few moments and he seems to be gathering his thoughts again, "Look, you're not looking out for your own interests."

"Bryn, you're full of shit!"

"Look," Bryn snorts, "when I told my brothers-in-law about you being a fag, they advocated violence against—"

"Oh, I'm a fag now! And what were you last night? You're uptight 'cause I fucked you. That's it isn't it?"

I can see Bryn's face grow red with anger. I see his hands tighten their grip on the wheel. "Look Neil, I'm trying to reason with you. My brothers-in-law told me that I should beat the shit out of you and leave you in a ditch somewhere," he says through clenched teeth.

"And is that what *you* think that you should do to me?"

Silence again.

"Bryn! Do *you* think that you should beat the crap out of me and leave me in a ditch somewhere!"

"They're. Just. Looking. Out. For. Me." He emphasizes every word as he squeezes them through his tightened lips. "Besides," he adds, "if you can't believe your family, then who can you believe?"

"Pee-yew! That's the worst piece of crap I've ever heard! They don't even know me. What makes you think that I give a shit what they think, anyway? I suppose they think a big, bad fag like me is going to turn a nice, innocent *straight boy* like you into some screaming queen! Should I get out the evening gowns and wigs? I roll down the car window and yell outside, 'Hey, everyone look at Bryn...'"

I feel the back of his hand give a firm warning hit to my chest. "Fuck off," he says.

"...doesn't he look cute in that chiffon number on the parade square?"

"Fuck you, asshole!" He gives me a firm swat to my chest while trying to keep control of the car. "Fuck right off!" Bryn shouts as he points his finger at me and shoots me with the arrows from his eyes.

"Oh, I'm real scared now. C'mon dickhead," I say, "pull over and I'll fuckin' deck ya!"

Bryn backs down. "You shouldn't have come on this trip," he snaps.

"Hey, bright boy, do I have to remind you again whose idea it was for me to come on this trip in the first place? What the fuck are you afraid of? Me? Or you?"

He continues to say nothing and watches the highway.

"I think this bullshit is just a cover-up, Bryn. I think that you're afraid of what you really are."

"Fuck you."

"Congratulations, that's the most real thing I've heard you say since we've hit the road this morning."

Bryn says nothing. I shake my head, turn from him and stare out the window. This whole situation is stupid. I glance back at him. I'm seeing a part of Bryn that I really don't like at all. I look at him while he's driving. I think of what happened last night, and all of the things that we've said to each other over the past few months. Why had I never seen this part of him before?

"It was a mistake for me to ask you to come," he says like a child trying to get a last word in. "I'm going on to Calgary alone."

"Yeah, you said that already."

Bryn shoots me a filthy look.

"Bryn, go to Calgary alone," I say, "if this is your reaction to my affection, then I'd rather be left in Winnipeg with my friends than be in Calgary with a guy who doesn't know what the fuck he wants."

"Well," he says, "I've already made arrangements for a room on the base in Moose Jaw only for me."

"Does it matter?"

There's a long strained silence in the car. I look at Bryn, who looks like he wants to say something.

"I like you, Neil. I really do, but I have to think about my family and my career too."

He seems to be waiting for a reaction from me but I'm silent.

"I didn't think you'd understand," he mumbles with a heavy sigh.

"No Bryn, I understand perfectly," I say. "I understand that you've told your family about me and they've freaked out. Now you're freaked out, and the sooner I'm out of the way, the more you can carry on this stupid straight game you're playing. Am I right?"

Bryn pulls the car over to the side of the road. He turns to me, looks me straight in the eyes, and says, "I can't afford to be with you, Neil. It's as simple as that."

The sudden intensity of his words sting me.

"Being with me has never bothered you before," I point out. "It didn't bother you the night that we went to that thing at the Officers Mess together. Remember that? That's when you told me how proud of me you were?"

Bryn turns and looks toward the road and says nothing.

"So you're telling me that you've planned to go to Calgary alone all along?"

"No Neil, I made arrangements for this room just this morning. I knew you'd be okay if I dropped you off with your friends in Winnipeg, and I'd continue on alone. I told them I would be in Moose Jaw tonight. So I'll drop you off in Winnipeg, and then drive on."

"And maybe you can tell me how you were planning to break this news to me? Or were you going to surprise me and just take off and leave me there?"

Bryn puts the car back into gear and pulls back onto the highway.

"I wasn't sure how I was going to tell you," he mutters.

I sink back in the seat. I feel like a sucker. I look at him driving.

"Bryn."

He looks at me out of the corner of his eye, "What?"

"You're a coward! What the fuck did I ever see in you? "

∞

Except for the sound of a Pink Floyd tape, a couple of silent hours have snailed by as we've continued along Highway 17 through Dryden and Kenora. Bryn's been watching the road and is acting like I'm no longer in the car with him. At this point I could give a shit. Any respect that I had for him has gone out the window.

I've been silent with my thoughts about this whole new twist of events. I've been watching the changing scenery and staring at the passing trees. The high clouds over the treetops look like brush-strokes on a light blue canvass. The sweet smell of the late-spring, northern Ontario forests have been filling my nostrils, as the wind from the open window has been running its fingers through my hair. I've calmed down and I've had a chance to think about what's gonna happen now.

Okay, I think, *obviously I'm not going to Calgary. Maybe I'll have a look at what's going on around Winnipeg. If nothing's going on there, then I'll move to Toronto and try to make a go of it, finally.*

It's then Bryn pipes up. "Look Neil, I'm sorry about the way I've behaved. I like you, I really do. I think you're a nice guy, and you deserve a nice guy to—"

"Yeah, yeah, spare me."

"Look Neil, I'm trying to make some peace between us. I don't want things to end on this kind of a note."

"Bryn, after everything that we've done together over the past few months, after everything we've said to each other, after knowing full well what the two of us have felt for each other, right from the night we met, there's nothing left to say after what you've done with this Moose Jaw bullshit. What kind of a cowardly bastard does this to somebody who's supposedly a friend? All I've ever wanted to do was to be with you. Go on! Go to Calgary alone—that's your choice—and if you can't handle being a fag that's for you to solve. I know I'm not the smartest guy in the world, but I ain't stupid. You, you're the one who's afraid of what people are gonna think. I'll be fine wherever I go and whatever I do because I know what I am, and I like it. You say that you don't want things to end on this kind of a note, but you're the one who's put an end to things, permanently. Fuck you, ya coward!"

∞

A couple of more hours have gone by on our drive from the Ontario border to Winnipeg, but it somehow seems like we've arrived in no time at all. The blacktop seems absolutely straight as we approach the city. We drive along the highway just east of the city and stop at a gas station. I get out and make a phone call to my friends Ron and Linda, while Bryn puts gas in the car. The phone booth is located outside, and at one corner of the building.

The sky is sort of half-sunshine and half thick, dark cloud just like in Thunder Bay yesterday. As I pick up the receiver and start to dial the number, I look out across the vast expanse of prairie. In the distance, I can see the office towers of Winnipeg's downtown. There are dark clouds quickly rolling over the city from the west, thunder rolls as they approach.

After four rings, Linda answers the phone, "Hello?"

"Hi, it's me."

"Neil! I've been waiting for your call all afternoon! Where are you calling from?"

"We're on the Trans-Canada Highway at a gas station just east of the city."

"Okay here's how to get to our place—got a pen?"

"It just so 'appens that I 'ave a pen *and* paper," I say with a mock-British accent. She gives me directions how to get to their place. I tell her that we'll arrive soon and I hang up the phone. I go back to the car just as rain starts to fall. Bryn says nothing and starts the car. We start to drive into the city, but before we know it we've driven into a downpour, and the rain drives so hard against the windshield that it blinds us. So Bryn pulls the car over to the side of the road, and we wait out the torrent. We don't have to wait too long, because as quickly as the storm hits, it moves on. We drive on.

We follow the directions that I've written on an envelope, and less than twenty minutes later we're driving down a side street in an older neighbourhood of town. The street's lined with brick and frame houses built near the turn of the century. Large trees stand majestically along either side of the avenue, hiding the homes from what's suddenly become a muggy late afternoon.

Linda has been keeping watch for us out of the living room window. I see her waving her arms frantically as she disappears from the window. As I step out of Le Car, she bolts out of the front door, barely touching any of the steps as she runs to me and we give each other a big hug and kiss. She's talking so excitedly that I can barely get a "hello" in edgewise. Introductions are made all around. Then after some pleasantries between us, Bryn and I take my gear out of the back of Le Car.

"This is great," says Linda barely containing herself. "We'll take you guys on a tour of the city tomorrow and—"

"I've actually gotta get on my way right now," Bryn interrupts.

Linda stops talking and looks really confused. "I thought that the both of you were staying for a couple of days."

"Something's come up," says Bryn. "I have to be in Moose Jaw by tonight, so I have to get on the road right away."

"Yeah, he's going on to Calgary alone," I say, casting an eye to Bryn.

Bryn's eyes sweep the pavement then he turns his head away from me.

I turn to Linda and I say, "I'll explain things to you later."

Linda approaches Bryn and says, "Are you sure that you can't stay for something to eat? You can stay for a couple of hours and still be there by tonight."

"No, thank you anyway. I really should be going."

"Okay," says Linda, "Um, maybe I should just let you guys say goodbye. It's been nice to meet you, if only for a few minutes."

"It's been nice meeting you as well," Bryn says forcing a polite smirk on his face.

Linda goes up the porch steps and disappears into the house.

As I pick my gear off of the sidewalk, Bryn comes over and tries to shake my hand. I stay still.

"Look, I don't want it to end like this, Neil."

I feel nothing toward him anymore. I feel no anger toward him, but there's no affection either. I look at him and I see a scared man.

"Bryn, one day you're gonna look in a mirror and see yourself for who you really are. Then maybe you'll have the guts to admit it. You're a fag, Bryn—a lyin' fag at that. You know it, and I know it. I said it before, the difference between you and me is that I'm happy with who I am. That's something you've gotta learn yet, and that's why you fuckin' lie about who you are. See ya, Bryn. Thanks for the lift to Winnipeg."

I turn and walk toward the house, shaking my head. As I climb the front steps to the veranda, I hear the door of Le Car slam shut. I slow my pace as I hear the engine start, and then I hear the car pull away. I tell myself that I won't watch him leave, but I turn my head in his direction just in time to see Le Car come to a stop at the corner, then make a left turn out of my life.

PART TWO

JULY 1979 - BRYN MENZIES

I don't know why I did it. All I know is that I wanted to get away from him. But he has been all I can think about since it happened yesterday. I didn't sleep very well last night, and with the driving that I've done today, I feel exhausted.

I pull into a gas station and coffee shop just off of the Trans-Canada Highway inside the eastern city limits of Calgary. I listen to the song on the tape as I sit in the car, watching the chaos of construction that's happening along the road in front of the station.

The heavy equipment whips up the early July dust, and the entire landscape is brown and dry. The wind creates small dust devils that dance around the road crew, deliberately kicking the baked earth in their faces. There must be thirty half-naked road workers stoically sweating in the late afternoon heat. I can't take my eyes off of them. I'm thinking about Neil again. I know that he'd make some kind of lewd comment about them.

I regret what happened between Neil and I on the way to Winnipeg. I wish he was here because I've got things I want to tell him. I'd tell him that the reason I didn't want him staying in my room that night back in Camp Borden was not because of the 10 o'clock curfew, but because I really wanted him to stay. That scared me. I especially liked the taste of his kiss, and the way his moustache tickled me when our lips met. That really scared me. But I guess it's too late for any of that now.

I snap out of my self-induced trance, and I realize I might be drawing attention to myself by sitting here motionless staring at the road crew.

I get out of the car and retreat to the coffee shop. I enter to the smell of fries and cigarette smoke and the din of country music. I buy a city map from the front counter and notice that most people are wearing white cowboy hats. A smiling, middle-aged woman takes my money. Her angular facial features, hooked nose and candy floss hairdo make me think of a plucked chicken. She asks me, "Where's your cowboy hat?"

"Is wearing a cowboy hat a necessity in this town?"

"During Stampede it is."

Oh right, the Calgary Stampede has just started.

"I forgot all about the Stampede. You see, I just moved here."

"Oh, where from?"

"Ontario."

"Welcome to Calgary."

"Thanks. I guess the first thing that I'll have to do is get a cowboy hat."

"That's the Calgary spirit," she says.

"I'm going to go inside for something cold to drink," I say pointing into the restaurant.

"Sure, what would you like?" she smiles.

"A large Coke would be great," I smile back.

"I'll bring it over to you," she says as she disappears into the kitchen.

I sit at a booth by a window that looks out at the road crew. I unfold the map and chart a route to the military base, which, as I examine the map, looks to be on the other side of the city. I plot a course through the streets of Calgary to Currie Barracks.

I notice this city is divided into four quadrants, Southwest, Northwest, Northeast, and Southeast, and already I can see where that may be confusing. I guess I'll have to be specific when looking for a particular address. And I'll have to remember to be careful to specify which quadrant I'm looking for. A chuckle passes my lips. Quadrant makes me think of Star Trek, which makes me think of Neil and our Captain Kirk routine.

The waitress interrupts my thoughts of Neil as she sets my Coke on the table in front of me. I thank her as she smiles and disappears once more. I look out the window to the road workers again.

I think of Neil and how he inspired me. I felt good about myself when I was around him. There was a confidence that came with that feeling, a confidence that I'd never known before.

I remember the night that I took him to that formal party at the Officers Mess back in Borden; I didn't care what the people in attendance were thinking. In fact, I had become so confident that I made up my mind I was going to tell my family about my being gay.

That morning on the road when I phoned my sisters from Kakabeka Falls I decided to float a trial balloon, and told them all about Neil being gay. I figured if they were cool with that, then I would tell them about me.

My sisters flipped right out. My brothers-in-law thought I should kick the shit out of Neil and leave him in a ditch somewhere. I didn't like that idea but I was silent.

All of those old insecurities came back to me, the secret infatuations that I felt for other guys at Royal Military College, the fantasies about them while I was alone in bed at night. I liked being sexually involved with women, but I always knew that I really wanted to be with another guy.

My family's reaction to Neil seemed to conjure all of the hate feelings that I've always had. I found that hard to handle. That's when I made up my mind that I wouldn't be completing the trip with him and made arrangements for that room in Moose Jaw last night.

Now I sit here, feeling more screwed up than ever because I now know that he's right. I am a coward, and it's that realization that hurts more than anything else.

My mind is blank, and the only sounds in the restaurant are the murmur of the other customers and a corny country song called *Heaven's Just A Sin Away,* blaring over the jukebox. I sit silently for a few minutes, going over what's taken place over the last little while. Then I decide it's time to get going.

I pay for my Coke then get back into the car, and proceed to crawl through Friday's traffic. I report at the Base and move my stuff into quarters in a little more than an hour. I sit on the naked mattress and I look at the four barren walls that seem to tower above me. My thoughts seem to echo through this disinfectant smelling room. My eyes scan its length and width. Every corner seems dark, even the large windows don't seem to bring much light in here. I hate it already. I feel so far away from everybody.

I get off the bed and open one of those windows. All's quiet, except the traffic noise on a busy thoroughfare not too far from this barrack block called Crowchild Trail. I have to laugh a bit. For all of the modern trappings of this city, they call all of their vehicle expressways "Trails." I guess they still think themselves a wild west town at heart.

I unpack my things and reach for my weekend bag. I unzip the side pocket and there is that copy of The Body Politic that Neil and I looked at before we got to Thunder Bay. I recoil in horror. I'd forgotten that I had put it there. Dammit what if somebody finds it here with me?

I snatch it from its resting place and something falls from between the pages and lands on the bed. It's that Polaroid that Neil gave to me. I find myself looking to see if anyone's around. Then I realize how stupid I'm being. There's nobody else in this room, and I'm just letting my fears get the better of me.

I look at the photo. There he is, laying on a couch not a stitch of clothes on, lit cigar in his mouth with his cock standing straight up to the camera. I lay back on the bed and stare at his image. That cigar reminds me of a turd hanging from his mouth. Suddenly the photo strikes me as funny; Neil with a turd in his mouth. A small giggle segues into laughter, and the more I try to stop myself, the harder I laugh. I look at the Polaroid again and I laugh even harder. I can't help it. I roll from side to side on the bed laughing hysterically. Tears run down my face, and my stomach's beginning to hurt from laughing so hard.

I eventually calm down and just lay still on the bed for a while. I get up to put the photo back in the newspaper, which I put back in my weekend bag. I set to work unpacking my things trying to make this place feel like home as much as I can.

∞

Unpacking took a little longer than I thought. I sit on the bed once more and yawn. With the driving from Saskatchewan and unpacking, I want to rest for a bit. I lay back on the bed and stare at the ceiling. I'm tired, but my mind is racing with thoughts of Neil once more. I had the chance to be with somebody who could have been my first serious relationship, and I really screwed him around. I've always liked guys—I can admit that—and Neil's right about my being a coward. I think about my family and how I let them control how I was feeling about Neil and my relationship with him. I guess all these years of my letting them determine what's best for me has made me a weakling. Then it occurs to me how right that is. I have been weak. And with that, a few other revelations strike me. It occurs to me that I'm now a couple of thousand miles away from my family. Do I have to worry about what they think about my friends, or about the life that I lead? Did I ever? Most of all, I wonder why I'd been so afraid of my sisters and their husbands finding out about my homosexuality. What were they going to do about it? Beat me up? Throw me out? I'm beginning to understand that I would have survived anything like that. Just being so far away from my family and lying here proves that to me. It's like being in a space where nobody can touch me. I go back to my weekend bag and pull out that copy of Body Politic once more. Neil's picture falls out again, so I pick it up and look at it. I put it in the drawer of the small night table beside the bed.

I open the paper and page through it. I look through the profiles of the various gay communities across Canada, and I stop when I get to the listings here in Calgary. I notice there's an organization called Gay Information Resources Calgary. The little written blurb says *information and counselling*. I guess that this would be the place to phone if I want to talk to somebody about this gay thing.

I jot down the phone number of the place because I'm not going to risk making any phone calls anywhere near the barracks. The only phone here is in the hallway. The last thing I need is for someone in barracks to overhear me talking to somebody about being gay. It occurs to me that here I am being worried about what people are going to think just when I promised myself that I wouldn't do that. But what the military doesn't know won't hurt me.

I'm hungry; no, I'm ravenous. Finding a restaurant is in order. This'll give me a chance to explore the city a bit. I go out to Le Car—I've gotta stop calling it that—and drive along Crowchild Trail with Steely Dan blaring from my cassette player. In seemingly no time at all I'm right downtown. It takes me about twenty minutes to find a parking spot because there are so many people downtown for Stampede. I turn a corner not too far from the Calgary Tower just on time to see a car pull out from a parking spot directly in front of me; I park the car and get out to have a look around.

Parents pushing children in strollers walk slowly by the line-ups of partiers trying to get into pubs and nightclubs. Traffic is almost at a stand still as Stampede revellers, bottles of beer in hand, hang out of cars yelling as loud as their inebriated voices will let them. Everywhere I look, these crowded sidewalks are a sea of white cowboy hats. I finally find a small restaurant on First Avenue South West that has a very short line up to get in. I've noticed a public payphone just around the corner. That's where I'll call this gay resource centre.

I get a small table in an out-of-the-way corner of the restaurant. This place is noisy and stuffy, so I order my meal, and when it comes I wolf it down. I pay for dinner and go outside to make the call.

I take the now crumpled piece of paper with the Resource Centre's number on it and go to the phone. I dial the number and a male voice answers.

"Gay Information Resources Calgary."

"Oh...um...you're still open?" I stupidly ask.

"Yes, sir."

"Okay. Umm, I'm new in town," I say in a low voice, "and I want to, you know, talk to somebody?"

"Well certainly, sir. You can—"

Just then a carload of particularly loud celebrants start beeping their horn and "yahooing" right outside the phone booth making it more difficult for me to hear.

"Sir, are you still there?"

"Sorry, I got distracted, I'm calling from a payphone downtown."

The voice on the other end laughs. Then asks, "If you're phoning from downtown, sir, where exactly are you phoning from?"

"Ah, hang on," I say and check a street sign nearby. "First Avenue Southwest. I can't make out what the cross-street is, but there's a railway overpass nearby."

The sounds from the street are drowning the voice on the phone.

"Okay," says the voice at the other end, "I think I know exactly where you are."

"If things are a little noisy there for you to hear me, we have a little drop-in centre here. Why don't you come over and we can talk here."

"Well I don't know."

"It's up to you, sir."

"Well, okay I'll come over then. How do I get there?"

"We're located in the Old Y Building, Room 312."

He gives me the address and directions how to get there.

"Okay, sir, I'll see you when you get here."

"Wait. What's your name?"

"Richard. And yours?"

"Bryn."

"Okay, see you when you get here, Bryn."

"Yeah, see you in a few."

Richard hangs up the phone. I hang up the phone and walk onto the street, following the directions Richard gave me. The early July evening is sunny and warm, and the street is buzzing with Stampede festivity. With every step I take, my heart seems to pound a little more.

I walk a couple blocks and find myself standing on the sidewalk in front of a majestic old brick building. It's three stories high, with a small, wide staircase that leads up to an old wood and glass double door. A sign across the top of the small box-like verandah welcomes you to the *OLD Y ACTION GROUPS*.

I can feel a knot in my gut. I want to go inside, but part of me wants to write this off as a bad idea and go back to the barracks. The palms of my hands have become so wet that I move them from my hips to inside my pants pockets.

Neil comes to mind once more. If he were here, he wouldn't think anything of going inside. Then I remember his parting words to me, *"You're a fag Bryn—a lyin' fag at that. The difference between you and me is that I'm happy with who I am. That's something you've gotta learn. That's why you fuckin' lie about who you are."* I feel those words like a kick in the ass. I run halfway up the stairs and instantly stop. I cautiously give a quick glance to either side of me, and hurriedly go inside.

The ceiling of this small lobby echoes with the faint voices of people in their offices down the halls to either side of me. A musty smell permeates this place as it seems to with most buildings of this vintage. An old flip chart facing the main entrance has *German Classes Tonight at 7:30 pm, Room 209* scrawled over it.

And then a wide staircase rises across from me. It moans, creaks and squeaks loudly with every step I take as it announces my arrival. I can hear the faint sound of voices mixed with Donna Summer singing *Bad Girls* as I approach the third floor. At the top of the stairs I face a wall sporting a sign with two arrows painted on it. The arrow pointing left tells me that Room 312 is that way, so I turn left down a short hallway. The music and male voices fill the empty corridor, and my heart pounds furiously as I approach the room. I can hear one shrill voice above the others saying, "Oh he's straight all right. Straight ta' bed!"

Uproarious laughter suddenly stops as I appear in the doorway. I see a group of guys sitting around a small, brightly painted lounge. They smile as I become the centre of attention.

"I'm looking for Richard," I smile nervously.

"Hey Richard!" yells a tall thin peroxide blond man sitting right next to the door.

"What!" yells somebody from another room.

"There's a good lookin' hunk out here to see ya!"

A dark-haired, broad-shouldered man appears from the other room. He has a huge, friendly smile. He's got a dark moustache and a brown cowboy hat. Judging from his complexion, he looks like he had a bad acne problem when he was a teenager.

"You must be Bryn," he shakes my hand.

"And you must be Richard."

"That's right, c'mon in."

"Richard, you're so rude! Introduce us to this good lookin' hunk," says the peroxide haired man.

Richard looks at me and smiles, "You really don't want to be introduced to these reprobates do you?"

I look at them and smile.

"Guys, this is Bryn and he's new in town."

I can feel my face turning red.

"Oh he's shy too. I like that in a man," says the peroxide blond.

"That's Howard," says Richard.

"Enchanté Monsieur." Howard extends his hand as an aristocratic woman would. This takes me aback. I go to shake his hand, but I hear the actor's voice in me. So I play along and kiss it.

"Oh a gentleman as well," he squeals.

"And this is Sparky." Richard points at a young guy with plastic framed glasses and a punk-style haircut. He's dressed in canary yellow pants, a white and black polka dot shirt and a dirty pair of runners.

"Hi!" says Sparky with a smile. I recognize his as the shrill voice from down the hall.

"This is Marcel." Richard indicates the fellow sitting beside Sparky on a large couch. Marcel puts down his cigarette, gets up, reaches over the small coffee table between us and we shake hands. His eyes penetrate me and he gives me a smile that seems to say, *I like what I see.*

"And this is Jim." Richard says pointing to a middle aged man with a beard, glasses and a white cowboy hat. He's too far for us to shake hands, so we smile and say hi to each other.

"Where are you from, you darling man," Howard asks, "since you're new in town?"

"Ontario."

"EEEEWWW!!" a couple of the guys chorus.

"You guys leave him alone," Marcel rushes to my defence. "Are you here for the Stampede, or are you looking for a job?" (I like that French accent of his).

"I'm in the Forces, and I've just been posted here."

"Oh I *knew* that he was a gentleman!" Howard flourishes as he fans himself with his hand. "I'm getting moist!"

The phone rings in the other room, so Richard excuses himself and goes to answer it.

"Why don't you join us?" Marcel smiles. He reminds me of Neil. He has a bit of a resemblance to him, although Marcel is shorter and thinner. But I like the way his eyes sparkle and his handsome face lights up. I sit between Marcel and Sparky.

"Marcel is Acadian from northern New Brunswick," says Howard with a smirk, "so sometimes it's hard to understand what he says."

Marcel points at Howard. "You kiss my be-harse!"

I laugh.

"Have you been in town long?" Sparky asks.

"I just arrived late this afternoon."

Jim pipes up, "You couldn't have landed in town during a better time than Stampede. This is the time of year when Calgarians just go nuts and party."

"We don't just party my dear," Howard jumps in, "we par-tay."

"What's the difference," asks Jim.

"My dear, if you have to ask…"

Richard emerges from the other room, "Okay everyone we have to evacuate the building."

"Oh, not another bomb threat," sighs Howard.

"I'm afraid so." Richard rolls his eyes.

"I'll start telling the other groups on this floor to abandon ship," says Sparky, practically leaping from where he's sitting.

Jim and Howard follow suit, "We'll take the second floor," says Jim as they disappear out the door and down the hall.

"C'mon," Marcel says, "we'll tell the groups on the main floor that they have to leave the building."

"I'll call the police and shut down everything here. I'll join you guys outside in a bit," Richard says as we rush out of the room and down the hallway to the staircase.

"Somebody's actually phoned in a bomb threat?" I ask Marcel as we fly down the stairs.

"Yeah it happens once in a while."

We reach the main floor, and Marcel knocks on the first door he comes to.

"You start over there," he points to a door across from us, "and work your way down the east hall. I'll go down the west hall."

I dutifully rush over to a door with a sign on it that says *The Weekend Social Group* and knock. A grandmotherly-type lady opens it and smiles. She's small in stature, well dressed and has a sticker on her sweater that says *Hello My Name is Edna*. The room is strewn with sewing material.

"Good evening ma'am," I say nervously, "we've had a bomb threat and everybody's going to have to leave the building right away."

"Oh dear," she says, "a bomb threat. That isn't very nice. Who sent a bomb threat to the building?"

"I don't know ma'am. I was just told—"

"Estelle," she turns to address two other ladies in the room, "did you here that? This nice young man has just received a bomb threat."

"Oh my goodness," one lady says, "what has he done to deserve that?"

"Oh are you one of those nice gay boys on the third floor?" asks the woman sitting beside Estelle.

I feel like there's a chicken bone caught in my throat and I try to speak but politely smile.

"I think that it's just terrible that somebody would deliberately want to hurt you folks," says Edna turning her attention back to me. "I have a granddaughter who's gay, and she's one of the most beautiful and friendly people that I know."

"I didn't know that you had a gay grand daughter," says the woman with Estelle.

"Oh yes," says Edna turning her attention back into the room.

"That's Brenda," says Estelle.

"Oh I like Brenda," says the woman with her.

"Is Brenda still living with that nice boy…oh what's his name, Ray? asks Estelle.

"His name isn't Ray, it's Martin," says Edna.

"Oh dear, for some reason I thought that his name was Ray."

"No Ray was the man that she was married to before she discovered she was gay."

"I guess I just don't understand how somebody can be married to a man and then decide that she's gay, but she's living with another man," muses the woman sitting with Estelle.

"Oh Martin is gay as well," says Edna "They're only roommates. She's happy with the living arrangements."

"Besides," says Estelle, "Maybe it was being married to a man that caused her to be gay,"

The three of them chuckle.

The sudden thunder of feet hurrying down the main staircase from the floors above sends a few volts of electricity through me.

"Um, excuse me ladies," I interject, "Maybe we should leave the building."

"Oh yes," says Edna, "I'll get my purse. Thank you for telling us young man."

As I move on, I glance to the front entrance and can see people already leaving the building. I approach an open door. In front of me, I see a young woman at a desk talking on the phone. I knock on the doorframe.

"Oh, just a moment," she says to the person on the line. She looks at me and says, "Yes?"

"We've just received a bomb threat and everyone's got to leave the building."

"Okay, thank you," she smiles. "I have to go now." I can hear her say to the person on the other end of the line as I leave the doorway.

I carry on to the next couple of doors, but there is no answer at either one of them. By this time I can hear more people coming down the main staircase and leaving the building. I continue to go door-to-door down this hallway getting people to leave.

I can see Marcel approaching me now. "Okay," he says, "I've finished the west hall, and you?"

"I knocked on every door I could see down this end."

"Okay, let's get out of here," he says as we leave the building.

A small crowd is gathered outside. Sparky, Howard, Jim, and Richard have already joined other people from the building as they wait for the police and fire department to arrive. As we join them, I smile at the three ladies from The Weekend Social Group who are presently talking with some of the others in the crowd. In the distance I can hear the approach of sirens.

The evening seems to have suddenly grown chilly, too cool to wear only a t-shirt.

"Are you okay?" asks Marcel with a warm smile.

"Yeah," I assure him, "just a little bit chilly, that's all. I didn't even bring a sweater."

"That's just nerves my dear," Howard chimes, "I felt the same way during my first bomb threat. It was in the middle of summer, on an evening much like this, and I was shivering like a dog shitting pineapples. What I wouldn't have given for the feel of my mink stole around my slender, gorgeous shoulders during that moment, (sigh) what a way to treat a lady."

A couple of women, who are standing near Howard, laugh. Jim is smiling at me. "Maybe now's a good time to go for Stampede drinks."

"What a splendid idea!" shrieks Howard, "Let's go to The Parkside, everyone's gonna be in a par-tay mood."

"I assume this Parkside is a gay bar?" I hesitantly ask.

"One of the three in town," Howard blinks his eyes at me.

I can feel that knot in my gut again. A gay bar. That's all I need is for somebody from the base to see me going into a gay bar.

"Hmmm, I don't know," I ponder.

"Oh c'mon," Howard encourages, "you don't mean to tell us that a brave officer in the military is afraid of a gay bar, do you?"

I politely give a nervous chuckle and look at the ground.

"Well Ah declare!," quips Howard like Scarlett O'Hara, "Why our Rhett Butler is afraid to go into a l'il ol' gay bah! And ah thought that ya'll were so brave and strong."

The sirens get louder as they get closer to us.

"I've never been to one before," I say a little annoyed. "You see I'm just, well this is all new to me."

"Why, ah do believe that our young officer is just coming out!" Howard flutters as he addresses the others in the group.

I feel deflated, like somebody's just discovered my darkest secret and announced it to the world. I can feel the blood flush from my face. I don't know how to answer.

"Really?" smiles Marcel with an evil sparkle in his eyes, "You're just coming out?"

By this time the sirens are overwhelming; two fire trucks pull up outside of the building then stop. The noise quickly fades to a moan then stops.

I feel marked. I look nervously at the people around us hoping they're not hearing any of this conversation. "Well I...I..." I stutter.

"Don't worry." Marcel smiles and winks. "We'll take good care of you." He puts his arm around my shoulder. I shudder in fear. I want to walk away. I quickly glance at the crowd around us again to see if anybody's staring.

"You guys go ahead to the Parkside," says Richard, "I have to stay behind and talk to the police. I'll catch up with you in a bit."

"Are you sure?" I ask wanting to put this off. "I don't mind staying behind."

"Bawk-bawk-bawk-bawk-bawk-BAWK!" mocks Howard.

"Look," I say defensively, "I think that someone should be here with Richard that's all."

"I can handle it, Bryn," Richard says, "this has happened before. I know what to do. You go on ahead, I'll see you in bit."

"Don't worry," Marcel smiles, "I'll protect you from any big bad fags who want to rape you."

Marcel looks me in the eye and a sly smile cuts across his face.

Reluctantly I go along with Marcel and the group as we head west for a block then cut across a beautiful park with a stately two storey stone and mortar building in the middle of it.

"Hey Bryn," Sparky says. "We're now entering one of the busiest spots in town."

"That's right," says Howard. "See those bushes surrounding that building? Wait'll it gets dark, my dear, you'll see a lot of man-to-man cruising going on."

"Right out in public like this? Aren't they afraid of getting caught."

"I believe our officer has led a rather sheltered life," observes Howard.

Marcel laughs, "You're so cute." He runs his hand up my arm. My body tenses. "What is that building anyway?" I ask to quickly change the subject.

"That's the old Carnegie Library," says Sparky. "But these days I think it's used as park administration offices."

We cross the street, following some disco music to a small club on a corner across from the park. The small marquee above the door says *Parkside Continental*; it's printed in a 1930's Hollywood type style. We form a small line at the entrance to pay a cover charge.

God I wish I were wearing a pair of sunglasses or some form of concealment. Then I notice this place has four, square windows along the wall that gaze out onto 4th Avenue South West. I don't like that at all.

"What if somebody sees us in here?" I ask Marcel pointing at the windows.

Marcel smiles and says, "Don't worry, they're like mirrors. We can see outside, but people outside can't see in."

The line is moving quickly and I'm just inside the vestibule when I can hear, "FAGGOTS!" being shouted from a passing car. My heart stops.

"BREEDERS!" is shouted back by somebody behind us.

We are buzzed through another pair of glass doors into the bar. The place is vibrating with the pulsing thumping bass of the music over the monitors.

There's an upper level of booths over to our left as we enter. I see both women and men milling around in high-spirits, and people of all ages are wearing cowboy hats of all colours.

The lights that flash above the small dance floor at the front of the room refract off the mirrors that surround it and back out over this crowded bar. The light show mesmerizes me. I look around me, through the dim light and the wafts of cigarette smoke; the dance floor is crowded and everybody's dancing and pounding their fists in the air in unison to the song playing on the loudspeakers.

There are men with their arms around each other kissing and necking like straight couples would, and women holding hands together, and not even glancing at any men who walk by them. I'm not used to seeing any of this type of thing at all. I feel like I'm in a foreign land, and yet I'm feeling like I've finally found home.

Jim bids us to follow him over to the upper level area and finds a couple of friends of his at a booth. The two of them make room for us, and I am introduced.

"Bryn, this is Frankie," says Jim indicating a broad-shouldered, middle-aged woman with boyishly bobbed, red hair. Her blue eyes are clear and sparkle, and she has the sweetest smile I've ever seen on anybody. She wears a plaid shirt with the sleeves rolled up to the elbow. "Hi," she says in a friendly tone as I shake her big calloused hands.

"And this is David Tøllin," says Jim as I reach across the table to shake hands with a handsome bearded man.

The waiter appears and a round of drinks is ordered. I have my scotch and water, Howard has a rum and coke, while everyone else at the table settles for beer.

"Bryn, that's an unusual name," David says. "What nationality is it?"

"Welsh."

"Are you Welsh?"

"My mother is, my father's people are from Scotland. I imagine that with a name like David Tøllin, you're Scandinavian."

"He's as Scandinavian as ABBA," interjects Jim.

"My father's from Sweden, and my mother is from Helsinki," David smiles.

We laugh.

I feel a hand squeeze my knee under the table. I turn to Marcel who's giving me a huge grin in between puffs on another cigarette. He smiles and says, "I want to be with you tonight." I smile back at him and nod. The thought of being physical with Marcel really excites me. I smile at him.

"Look, why don't we go back to your place?" I suggest.

"We can't go back to my place," says Marcel.

"Why not?"

"My roommate's ex-girlfriend has shown up unexpectedly for Stampede."

"What's that got to do with us?"

"Well, she's kind of invited herself over to our place to stay with us while she's here from Saskatoon. She's trying to get back together with him but she doesn't know that he's gay. So he wanted to be alone with her tonight to tell her. Who knows what kind of a scene we may be walking into."

"Well where do you suggest that we go then because we can't go back to my barrack block?"

"Oh, I know a place where we can be together. Trust me."

Okay, I think.

"I've never seen you around before, Bryn," Frankie says. "You here for the Stampede?"

"No, I've just moved here."

"Oh, where from?"

"Ontario."

"EEEWWW," she smiles and winks.

"Frankie is a ranch dyke from up near Red Deer," says Howard.

"That's right," she says, "and I'm gonna get Howie up there to break in one of my steers."

"No way sister," smiles Howard.

"So help me Howie you're goin' on my prize bull!"

"Not unless you can supply me with a side saddle and a manicurist, girl. After all I am a lifetime member of the Imperial Order of the Daughters of the Empire."

Frankie breaks into a loud belly laugh. Then she cranes her neck and squints in the direction of the front entrance.

"Are they here?" David asks.

"Yep. Could you send the waiter over with my beer?" she asks David. David agrees. "It was good to meet you," Frankie says excusing herself.

"Good to meet you too," I smile. "And I hope to see you again."

"Well you've got to come out to the ranch to see Howie on that steer," she smiles and winks.

"Oh God, girl," Howard sighs.

Frankie laughs, she goes over to a group of women that have just walked through the door. "Frankie!" yells one of the group as they give each other a big kiss.

I turn to look at David. "That's Frankie's new love," he says.

My attention goes back to Jim, Sparky, and Howard who are talking about plans for a national Gay and Lesbian convention next year. Judging from their conversation, it sounds like it's going to be here in Calgary. Marcel and I sit quietly. Every once in a while he will glance at me and wink, and I nod and smile in return.

∞

I look at my watch. It's 1:00 am and only Marcel and I are left at the table. Sparky, David, and Jim went off to a stampede party a couple of hours ago, and Howard was tired so he went home. Frankie waved at us as she left with her lover and group of friends.

Around us is a vortex of loud disco music and drunken laughter. I'm shocked by the sight of a blowjob taking place at one of the neighbouring booths. Without any reservation a guy is sitting at the booth watching as his buddy goes down on him as if nobody else is in the room. A bouncer appears and orders the guys to get out now! The one guy zips up his pants and the two of them silently leave.

"Did you see that?" I ask Marcel.

"Those two do that all the time," Marcel smiles. "It's a wonder they haven't been permanently banned from this place yet."

I watch the two of them being followed by the bouncer as they exit the door, and in an instant they're gone.

Marcel reaches across the table and cups his hands around mine. "You ready to go?" he smiles.

I smile back and nod my head.

We leave the Parkside, and I take a quick, cautious glance around us as we exit the building. We walk to Second Street and Seventeenth Avenue South West where Marcel leads me into a small parking lot behind a couple of small buildings. An eight-storey apartment building looks down onto us, and somewhere on one of the top floors a party is in progress. I can see a handful of people on a balcony silhouetted against the lights from the living room. Laughter and music swirl from the apartment above, and scatter through this parking lot like autumn leaves in a whirlwind.

I follow him to a small ramp leading to a door in the basement of a one-storey building.

"What's this place?"

"Have you ever heard of a steam bath?"

I stop cold. These are the places where gay guys go to have sex with other men. I've heard horror stories from other cities of these places getting raided by the police. Being caught inside of a gay bath-house is the last thing that I need. I can see newspaper headlines screaming, "MILITARY OFFICER CAUGHT IN HOMOSEXUAL STEAM BATH!"

"No way Marcel," I assert, "I'm not going in there."

Marcel looks confused, "What's the matter?"

I move closer to him, "I don't want my career to end especially when it's only just beginning," I whisper.

"What do you mean?"

"What if somebody from the Base sees me going in there with you? What if I'm recognized?"

The confusion drains from his face and no emotion takes it's place. He folds his arms, "I thought you said you were new in town," he says.

"Well I am. So?"

"So who the hell is going to recognize you?"

"I don't know, guys at the Base I guess."

"Who do you know there that would recognize you?"

I hesitate then say. "That's not the point."

"So what is the point?"

"Well, I mean, what if the cops decide to raid it?"

Marcel looks away from me for an instant, then looks back at me. "You're full of excuses. What are you afraid of? Me? Or you?"

I don't know if it's me, the scotch or just the way that Marcel said that, but it dawns on me that Neil said those exact words.

Marcel unfolds his arms and brings out a small pad of paper and a pen from one of his shirt pockets.

"It's been a long day for you," he says as he scribbles something on it, tears off the page and hands it to me. "Maybe you should go back to the barracks and get some sleep. Call me later this weekend." He turns and walks away.

I look at the paper to see his name and phone number on it. I watch him as he walks further from me. I'm not sure what it is, but something inside snaps and I find myself running after him. "Marcel!" I yell, then I trip and land on the boulevard grass.

In an instant Marcel is crouched beside me with his hand on my shoulder.

"Are you okay?"

I nod my head and say, "I don't want to go back to the barracks to be alone. I want to be with you tonight."

"Well c'mon inside asshole," he says, "don't be afraid. Nobody'll bite. But they might just lick around the edges."

I get up and look in the direction of the steam bath. "Well, I don't know," I say.

"Bryn, you're being foolish," Marcel says matter-of-factly. "Nobody's gonna recognize you and the cops aren't gonna raid the place. Now c'mon."

We go back, walk down that small ramp in the parking lot, and enter the building's basement. My eyes dart around the lot to see if anybody's watching us go inside. We are in a small vestibule, and immediately to our right is a good-looking guy behind a small window.

"Hi guys," he says not bothering to look at us as he writes something in a notebook.

"Hi," replies Marcel.

"If you guys want a room, there is about a twenty minute wait. In the meantime, lockers are eight dollars each."

"Okay," Marcel says.

We're buzzed through a heavy locked door, to a small countertop. We pay him eight dollars each and he hands us two folded white towels. We're handed a pen and a slip of paper each. The paper says I have to fill out my name address and phone number for a membership list.

Marcel is busy filling out the slip of paper while I stare at it like it has landed in front of me directly from the moon. Marcel notices me and whispers in my ear, "Make up a name and use my address." I stare at the slip of paper once more then write *Charles Dickens* in the name column. Marcel puts his slip of paper in front of me and I copy his address and phone number in the appropriate places.

We hand the papers back and step into a hallway. The sight of men—of all shapes and sizes—wearing nothing but white towels greets us. I follow Marcel as we make a left turn into a locker room.

A local radio station is being played loudly over the speaker system, which is interspersed by announcements like, "Locker 19, we have a room ready for you. Locker 19, a room is ready for you."

We go to our lockers, and to my left a young, skinny, clean-shaven guy is struggling with a red and white Adidas bag that he has stuffed into one of the smaller lockers. He finally yanks the bag out of the locker spilling its contents all over the floor.

"Fuckin' useless God damned piece of shit," he mutters as he throws the spilled contents back into the bag.

To my right, a slightly overweight, bearded guy smiles, and looks me up and down as he wraps his towel around his waist. "Have a good time tonight," he says as he pats my ass and disappears down a hallway crowded by other towel-clad guys. I look back to Marcel who has already shed the shirt that he was wearing and put it in his locker.

"C'mon Bryn, take your clothes off and relax," he says smiling.

I slowly disrobe and wrap the towel around me. Marcel stands in front of me and runs his hands up my arms. "I've never been with a red-haired man before," he says. He runs two of his fingers along my upper lip. "And you have a beautiful red moustache, it's so soft." He kisses me. I close my eyes and feel like my feet are melting through the floor. He puts his arms around me and I immediately embrace him.

"Let's go for a shower," he winks.

I nod my head and follow him down a hallway, making a right, then left turn into the shower area. An older man smiles at us and looks us up and down. Not being sure about bathhouse etiquette I politely smile back. We put our towels on a couple of hooks, then Marcel runs a shower and I do the same.

I'm barely wet when Marcel joins me under the shower. He rubs his hands up and down my chest.

"You have a beautiful body," he says. "Do you go to the gym a lot?"

"I swim a lot," I answer, "and I like to jog." I am feeling slightly embarrassed by his compliment.

Then Marcel kisses me deeply. I close my eyes and start to get into it with him, when I can feel another hand on my back. Marcel and I turn at the same time to see the older man smiling wanting to join us. He immediately plants a big, sloppy kiss on my mouth.

Marcel pushes him back a bit, "Whoa tiger, this is a private party."

The guy looks disgusted. "Well get a fuckin' room then," he says abruptly removing his hands from us.

"We're waiting for one, asshole," Marcel retorts.

The guy snaps his towel from a hook, shoots daggers at us from his eyes and storms out of the shower area. Marcel looks back to me and says, "Forget him. Now where were we again?" We kiss once more, and those kisses get deeper by the second.

I've never felt an intense sensation like this ever in my life. Holding Marcel's naked body against mine with the warm water rushing over us, I'm suddenly in another world where nobody or nothing else exists.

Then I become aware that more people have entered the shower area. Marcel pushes himself back from me. "Let's save this until we get a room," he says. I agree.

"C'mon," he says, "I'll show you around."

We dry ourselves off while the three spectators who were expecting a show leave the shower room. We wrap our towels around ourselves once more, and I follow Marcel out and around a corner to a small hallway. I peer into a small area with a jacuzzi. There's not a soul in here. Probably because the jacuzzi looks like it hasn't been cleaned in God knows how long. It looks like there's a film or scum floating on the surface. I feel my face screw up in disgust. We move on.

Down a narrow hallway with a row of doors to my right, every guy we pass stops to look me up and down. My eyes dart from right to left as I try to ignore their sly smiles and avoid making eye contact with them. But I feel like I'm the main course being served to a bunch of hungry patrons at a banquet. Is this what a woman feels like anytime she passes by a group of guys? We turn left into a small lounge.

Table lamps cast a dim light while a couple of old men sit on a couch drinking coffee. Elizabeth Taylor is playing super bitch as Who's Afraid of Virginia Wolfe blares from the television.

"This is one of my favourite movies," smiles Marcel. "As far as I'm concerned only a gay guy could write a script as bitchy as this."

I chuckle. Then Marcel leads me back down the hall until we reach a set of stairs leading down to a darkened doorway. A couple of guys stand at the entrance staring into the blackness of the room. An almost steady stream of guys flows in and out of the darkness. The two guys watch us as we descend the stairs and stare into the invisibility.

Shadows are barely noticeable as I can only see about three feet into the room, and all is as quiet as a church.

"Why is everyone so quiet?" I whisper to Marcel.

"They're busy," he smiles back at me.

"But I can't see anything in there."

"You're not supposed to *see* anything, you're supposed to *feel* them."

Just then, the slightly over weight, bearded guy from the locker room emerges from the darkness. His face lights up as he sees me. He smiles, squeezes my left nipple, and glances behind him as he climbs the stairs. He licks his lips at me and motions me to follow him.

I look at Marcel who is really enjoying watching my reactions to everything. He smiles and says, "Just stay with me."

An announcement comes over the PA system, "Locker number 23, we have a room for you. Locker number 23, we have a room available for you."

"That's me," Marcel smiles. He takes my hand and leads me back to the place we started from. He goes to his locker and removes his things from it. I follow suit.

"No, keep your clothes in your locker," he says, "there's only supposed to be one person to a room."

"Well what am I supposed to do then?"

"Just follow me."

Then he goes to the fellow behind the small counter and turns in his locker key. His valuables are put in a small safety box; which is kept behind the counter, and another key is issued to him

Marcel takes the key and his clothes then bids me to follow him down the hallway to room #7. We go in and Marcel closes the door. He hangs his clothes on a hook then he kisses me again. His kissing takes on a passion that he hasn't shown me until now. It's like our lips are glued together—all I can feel are his lips against mine, and the two of us are getting aroused. This feeling comes over me like a tidal wave, and I just let all of that pent up frustration go. I pull his towel from his body, and he pulls mine from me. We fall onto the small bed.

∞

The music over the PA system fades and then suddenly seems to yell in my ears as I drift between sleep and semi-consciousness. I'm startled awake to a slapping sound in the next room. A steady slapping sound with some guy's voice repeating, "Yes, sir! Yes, sir!" in between slaps.

What kind of weirdness is this? I think. I look toward the sound of the slaps, and try to settle back down snuggling into Marcel. I close my eyes and get a picture in my mind. A sadistic commanding officer with a naked corporal kneeling in front of him administers this kind of punishment for insubordination. I open my eyes again. The slapping and the slavish response continue. I wonder how anybody could find this sexually arousing.

Marcel lies beside me with his eyes closed. He doesn't seem to be bothered by the slaps. In fact, his feet start to bounce in rhythm to

Mama Can't Buy You Love by Elton John playing over the PA system. I hold him closer and kiss him. He opens his eyes and smiles.

"Doesn't that bother you?" I ask.

"No, I like Elton John"

"Not the music, that slapping."

Marcel shrugs his shoulders and continues to bounce his feet in rhythm.

I look at him and smile, then I shut my eyes and snuggle beside him again as the slapping stops.

∞

It's 7:00 in the morning as Marcel and I exit the steam bath. The sun is up and almost stings my eyes. Not having slept very well for the second night in a row, I'm too tired to care if someone sees me coming out of the building.

"Come over to my place for coffee," says Marcel.

"I thought we couldn't go back to your place because of your roommate's ex-girlfriend."

"That was last night," Marcel assures me.

"In that case I could go for a coffee," I agree.

The side streets are empty as we make our way back to the place where I parked my car. The birds sing their wake-up calls from the Cottonwood trees that shade the sidewalks. The storefronts are silent, and the small apartment buildings that we pass seem to be asleep themselves.

A lone figure walking a Bassett Hound rounds the corner in front of us. His hair is disheveled, his face unshaven, and he wears a pair of sandals, cut-offs and a black t-shirt. He holds the dog leash in his left hand and a cigarette between two fingers in his right. His eyes hang tiredly.

Marcel bends down to pet the dog.

"What's your dog's name?" he asks.

"Blue," yawns the guy.

"Hey Blue. How are ya doin' girl?"

Blue wags her tail and licks Marcel's hand.

The guy yawns again then says to himself, "C'mon Tom wake up. You've gotta be at work in a couple of hours."

"Oh a couple of cups of coffee and a shower will fix that," I say.

He nods his head in agreement, "Coffee," he says, "that's what I need. Coffee."

"Well," says Marcel getting up, "We'd better let you get on you way. Have a good one at work."

Tom yawns for a third time while waving a pleasant return to us.

We walk to the park that we cut across last night to go to the Parkside. We enter the park to the sorry sight of a clump of wasted humanity passed out at the foot of a Cenotaph. He clutches an empty bottle to his chest, and it's hard to see his face because of the way he's laying. The dirty clothes that hang lifelessly from his body make him look like a big discarded old dishrag.

Marcel looks away from him. "I wonder what drove him to that condition," he says.

I shake my head and say nothing. We walk on.

We walk by the Old Y building where the bomb threat was last night, under a railroad bridge, and finally to my car. It's a good thing we've arrived when we have because I now see a sign telling me that my parked car should have been out of here an hour ago. I'm glad it hasn't been towed yet, but I pick the yellow parking ticket from the windshield and look at it. Fifty bucks for a parking ticket. I roll my eyes and mumble, "Welcome to Calgary."

I realize that I'm too tired to drive. "Marcel, do you drive?" I whine.

"Sure, I'll drive if you want me to," he smiles as I hand him my car keys. He unlocks the car, climbs into the driver's seat, and unlocks the passenger door. I climb in, do up my seatbelt, close the door, and toss the ticket in the glove compartment. Then I fold my arms across my chest and shut my eyes. Marcel starts the ignition.

I'm aware the car is in motion, and as we pull out of the parking spot and begin driving down the street, my mind drifts. I see that vision of the commanding officer and the naked corporal again. I open my eyes as we're driving on a bridge over a river. It looks like we're heading out of the city centre.

"Where do you live?" I ask him.

"An area of town called Bridgeland," he says. He turns to me and smiles. "We're almost at my place now." I shut my eyes once more, and no sooner do so than I feel the car come to a halt, and the engine is turned off.

"We're here," he says looking at me once more.

In my bleary state I look onto the scene. Both sides of the street are lined with cottonwood trees that attempt to hide the wooden houses; which were probably built about fifty years ago. A large grassy hill rises at the end of the street with a sprawling brick building atop it. It seems to dwarf every other building in the area. As I get out of the car, I examine it. "What is that place," I ask.

"It's Calgary General Hospital."

We lock the car, and I follow Marcel to a small, white, one-storey house. He hands me back my car keys as he opens the gate, and I follow him down a narrow sidewalk between houses to the back door. I see the remnants of a garden in a corner of the small overgrown yard. Two kids are already playing in the yard next door. Their backdoor suddenly flies open.

"You Goddamn kids get in this house right now!" I hear a voice demand.

"Aaaawww," groans one of the children.

"Never mind that get your asses in here right now!"

The kids slowly climb the stairs back into their house. The door slams shut behind them, and I hear the muffled scolds from, I assume, their father.

Marcel unlocks the door and we go inside his place.

A small but brightly painted kitchen greets me. The smell of freshly brewed coffee along with a slight hint of gas from the ancient stove in the corner caresses my nose. A good-looking, clean-shaven guy sits at the old chrome trimmed kitchen table. He looks up from his reading and acknowledges us.

"Bryn, this is Vince. Vince this is Bryn," Marcel introduces us. Vince and I shake hands.

"How did it go?" Marcel asks Vince.

He shrugs and says, "Okay, I guess."

"Is Shelley still asleep?"

"No, she's in the living room watching cartoons."

I hear a crunching sound to my right. I look down to see a big orange tabby cat munching on some food.

"That's Tenacious," says Marcel.

"Tenacious?" I respond.

"Yeah, we call him that because he is," replies Vince.

Marcel goes to the coffee pot. "What do you take in your coffee?" he asks retrieving two mugs from the paint-chipped cupboard.

"Cream, no sugar," I reply.

He prepares the coffee, hands a mug to me and bids me to follow him. We step down into a long dark hallway. I catch a glimpse of the bathroom through the open door immediately to my left. There's a closed door on my immediate right, and another one beside the bathroom door. I catch another quick glimpse of an unmade bed with a couple of piles of clothes on the floor beside it through the next open door to my right. Then we walk into a small living room.

The room is full of cigarette smoke as a woman with long brunette hair is glued to the TV. She's wearing a faded cream coloured night shirt, and the couch she sits on is strewn with bed sheets, two pillows and a blanket. She rests her cigarette on the ash try and sips her coffee.

"Shelley, this is Bryn," says Marcel, "Bryn this is Shelley."

"Hello," I say extending my hand to her.

"Hello," she responds turning her attention back to the television. I glance at the TV and Porky Pig is dressed like Friar Tuck while Daffy Duck is playing Robin Hood.

"Have a seat," Marcel says to me. "I'll be right back." He disappears down the hall into the bathroom.

I sit on an old green overstuffed chair with a worn-out throw covering it. I can see from the condition of it that Tenacious likes to use it as a scratch post.

I look over to Shelley. "So Marcel tells me you're from Saskatoon," I say trying to strike up a conversation.

Her back stiffens as she inhales deeply and says, "That's right." She doesn't look at me.

Silence.

"Are you going to visit that Stampede while you're here?"

She takes another deep breath and quickly turns to me with a forced smile and says, "Yes." She looks back to the TV.

I look back to the television.

Daffy Duck is poised on the branch of a tree with a vine in his hand trying to prove to Friar Tuck that he's Robin Hood. "YOIKS! AND AWAY!" He yells as he swings on the vine and slams headlong into a tree trunk. He staggers onto the next branch. "YOIKS! AND AWAY!" He yells once more as he swings into another tree trunk. I burst out laughing while Shelley turns her head slightly and glares at me. Now sounding punch drunk, Daffy yells, "YOIKS...AND AWAY! " while still swinging and still slamming into tree trunks. I can't contain my laughter. Shelley turns her back to me.

∞

I wake up and have to think about where I am for a moment. Oh yeah, I'm in Marcel's room. I glance over to the clock on the bedside table. It is 1:05 pm. We only came to bed to lay down for half an hour and that was four hours ago.

The sun pours around the nearly worn canvas blind pulled over the window, like a corona around an eclipsed sun. In the afternoon light my eyes quickly sweep the room.

I look at the foot of the bed and see a ten-speed bike resting lazily against the wall. Clothes are carelessly strewn over it like rumpled sheets as if it were in bed sleeping. An antique wardrobe majestically towers over the room from its corner. Its full-length mirror reflects the eclipsed sunlight making the room appear brighter. There's life outside as I hear the sound of the children in the backyard next door once more.

Beyond the closed bedroom door all seems silent in the house. I wonder if Shelley and Vince have gone out. I look over to Marcel. He looks peaceful as he lays beside me with his eyes closed. His dark moustache droops over his open mouth while his brows form an almost complete arc over his eyes. He looks like he's far away. I lightly kiss his cheek. His face twitches a bit and then returns to sleep.

I smile. I'm thinking about the events of the last 24 hours. It's funny how life can so quickly turn. This time yesterday I hadn't even arrived in Calgary, and I knew nobody. Then I have a revelation and decide to phone that Gay line number just to talk to somebody, now here I am lying beside Marcel in his bedroom. This feels so good, and I can't understand why I've run from this for so much of my life. Then I think of Neil again and for a moment I wish that it was him laying here with me.

Hey Neil, I think, *if you could only see me now. No more fear. No more fear.*

"Jeez, maybe I *can* do anything I want to," I say under my breath.

"Who said you couldn't?" answers Marcel startling me. "Caught ya," he grins, "You were thinking, and thinking's dangerous."

I laugh and say, "So what are you going to do about it?"

Marcel quickly throws the covers off me, plants his mouth on my belly and blows, making a big farting sound. I laugh hysterically. It tickles. I thrash from side to side in hysterics. Marcel's mouth is still firmly planted on my belly and he's still blowing on it making a chorus of loud fart noises.

He stops and brings his mouth to mine. We kiss. I hold him closer to me as our kisses become deeper. The phone in the kitchen rings. It rings again, and for a third time. Then somebody picks it up and I hear Vince say, "Hello…"

Marcel and I continue to kiss, when a knock comes to the door, "Marcel," Vince says, "Frankie wants to talk to you."

He smiles and winks at me. "I'll be right back," he says as he gets up, puts a housecoat on and goes into the kitchen. I lay my head back on the pillow and look at the ceiling. I can barely hear the muffled conversation Marcel is having with Frankie.

I'm disturbed by a small thud. I look toward the foot of the bed to see Tenacious giving me a look that says, *Who the hell are you, and what are you doing here?*

"Hey Tenacious," I smile, "How ya doing?"

Tenacious gives me a disgusted snort and jumps off the bed just as I hear Marcel hanging up the phone. Marcel comes back into the room, takes off his housecoat, throws it across the foot of the bed, and climbs back in beside me.

"Frankie wants you and me to go with her and her friends out to a Stampede party tonight," he says. "I think it would be fun, it's going to be the party of the summer. Everybody's going to be there."

"Well," I hesitate, "the barracks."

"What about it?"

"I haven't been there since yesterday evening, and I really should spend some time unpacking more boxes. Although I hate like hell the thought of even going back there."

"Why?"

"It's feels so bloody empty."

"Once you're unpacked it'll look more lived in."

"That's not what I mean."

Marcel has a puzzled look on his face.

"Look Marcel, when I'm in that room I'm reminded of how lonely I feel, that's all."

Marcel ponders for a moment. "Well the answer is simple," he says.

"And what's that?"

"Don't finish unpacking."

"Pfff, yeah right," I say.

"Is there a rule that you have to live in barracks?"

"Well, no."

"When is your first day of duty?"

"In about a week and a half I guess."

"Great! Then we'll spend a few days looking for an apartment for you. How does that sound?"

Hearing Marcel saying that comes as yet another revelation.

Even though Neil and I talked about it, I never thought of getting an apartment off the base, at least not by myself, "That would make life a whole lot easier for me," I say. "I guess Calgary is a big enough city that I can be with the people I want to be with when I'm off duty, and still keep my work life separate."

I laugh. "Hey I'm really starting to like Calgary."

"So what about that party tonight?"

"I guess we're going," I say with a smile.

Marcel leaps on me growling like a bear and tickling the side of my belly. I laugh again. Then Vince knocks on the door.

"Will you two settle down, I'm trying to study."

∞

What a place! This house is only a small cottage, but the backyard is huge, and I swear there must be well over one hundred people here. There might even be close to two hundred! A sea of cowboy hats and western shirts surrounds the place, and I feel naked not having worn anything cowboy–like. My eyes dart from side to side and back again as I try to take everything in at the same time.

Bright patio lanterns are strung from the back porch, through the tree branches that surround the yard, making a full circle to the back porch. Men and women are laughing and talking loudly to be heard. The music blares over the speakers set at either side of the porch, while a group of guys off to my right are singing drunkenly along to the chorus of Nick Lowe's *Cruel to be Kind.*

We arrived with Frankie, but she has disappeared into the crowd somewhere, and I'm hearing snippets of passing conversation as Marcel and I wade deeper into the crowd.—Oh I don't know what he wants, and I don't think he does either

—You guys should really go, I know you'd love it there

—She'll be graduating from high school next year. Where has the time gone?

—The only bad thing about this new job is that I have to move up to Edmonton

—Oh he's in the military so he's a closet case

I quickly turn my head in the direction I think that last remark came from. I feel like I've been pointed out. But just then I hear one guy's voice above the others say, "Hey Patrick! What word comes after Calgary!" A drunken voice somewhere else in the crowd yells back, "STAAAMMMMPEEEDE!" A holler goes up from almost the entire crowd. I chuckle because this is like no party I've ever been to before. This type of behaviour would never happen at any party in staid old Ontario.

"You haven't met the hosts of the party yet, have you?" Marcel asks as he nudges my arm.

"I guess not."

"Well come on," Marcel says grabbing my hand as we squeeze through the crowd. On our way I make eye contact with David Tollin. I swear I see a flash of light from those eyes of his as he gives me a warm smile and interrupts his conversation. I return the smile. As we slowly shuffle by, David says, "Hi Bryn."

"Hi David."

"Did you just arrive?"

"Yeah."

"How are you?"

"Still a bit tired, but okay."

"We'll talk a bit later."

"Right, I'll catch you later."

We find our way over to a group of people clustered around a table full of food. Marcel approaches a tall, thin man from behind and taps him on the shoulder. He turns around. He looks like he is in his forties and has a very thin face with dark eyes and a large nose. His thin, shoulder-length hair is cut in bangs across his forehead, and his wispy beard make me think of what a Charles Dickens character might look like.

"Marcel!" he smiles as he picks Marcel up off the ground and gives him a hug. "I haven't seen you in a while. What have you been up to?" Speaking of Dickens, he has a thick British accent.

Marcel puts his hand on my arm and says, "I've been up to him."

"Oh, he *is* a looker," he smiles at me.

"My name is Bryn," I smile extending my hand to him.

"Ohhh, a good Welsh name," he says. "I'm Tony, but you might as well call me Honker, everybody else does."

It's only then that I notice the bright yellow t-shirt he's wearing with the words *Big Nose* emblazoned across his chest in red letters.

"Bryn's just moved here from Ontario," Marcel says.

"Oh," smiles Honker, "welcome to Calgary."

"Thank you. This is quite a party. I like how everybody just seems to cut loose."

Honker laughs, "Well, I can tell you that in England we never had parties where the whole crowd would holler like this one just did. This must be your first Stampede then."

"It's that obvious is it?"

"I'm afraid so." Honker continues, "So are you of Welsh ancestry?"

"My mother's people are from Wales," I answer, "and my father's people are from Scotland. What part of England are you from?"

"I'm Geordie," he answers. "I'm from the north around Newcastle-On-Tyne."

"Well you're not too far from Hadrian's Wall then."

"Not too far indeed, not too far indeed."

"Where's Mark?" asks Marcel.

Honker quickly scans the crowd and says, "I think he actually went inside to get more paper plates. Ah, there he comes now."

A bespectacled younger man emerges from the crowd carrying four packages of paper plates. He is clean-shaven and sports a white straw cowboy hat. Marcel looks at me and says, "Mark and Honker have been together for eleven years."

"Bryn," says Honker, "this is Mark."

Mark and I shake hands and greet each other. Just then a loud cheer, laughter and applause go up from the crowd at the far end of the yard. I can't see what's happened because the crowd is so thick. But somehow above the din I hear Frankie's voice yelling, "Howie was you doin' the hula-hula when I wasn't lookin'!"

"How's your drink?" Mark asks me.

"Oh, my Scotch is fine for now, thank you."

"Please help yourself to some food, there's lots here."

Before I can get the words 'thank you' out of my mouth, I see a really tall woman coming through the crowd toward the food table. She has a red sequined western hat that seems to dangle precariously from atop a white beehive hairdo, with a pair of rhinestone, cats-eye sunglasses peering from underneath. She sports a white blouse with a multi-coloured plastic Hawaiian lei around her neck, and a red sequined vest with a long grass skirt. She smiles.

"Hello my dear soldier boy," she says.

"Howard, is that you?" I ask.

"I am NOT Howard. I am the Prairie Princess Wannalaya."

"The Prairie, what?" I chuckle.

"He's been this way ever since his trip to Honolulu two Christmases ago," Marcel says.

"Your Highness," bows Mark.

"Arise, Sir Milk of Magnesia," answers Howard.

127

"And were you doing the hula-hula when Frankie wasn't looking?" Honker asks.

"Off with his head," says Howard pointing at him, "who cares about Frankie when everybody *else* was looking. And besides, my kingdom is not Honolulu, it's Homolulu," he sniffs indignantly.

I look down to Howard's feet to see he's wearing a pair of red sequined platform shoes. "Those are really nice Elton John shoes you're wearing," I say and snigger once more.

"As any girl like Elton knows," Howard responds, " a good pair of high heels and the world is yours."

I look at Marcel. We both smile and shrug our shoulders.

"Would Her Highness care for some food?" asks Mark.

"Oh, there are gentlemen left in this town. Kindly fill my plate my good sir."

"You know on second thought," I say to Marcel, "maybe I will have a top up on my Scotch after all."

"I'll go inside and get you one," he says taking my drink and disappearing into the house.

"Bryn have you been to the Stampede yet?" Honker asks.

"No," answers Howard on my behalf, "Our chivalrous knight only arrived yesterday."

Just then I feel a pair of arms wrap around my chest from behind. My back stiffens as I look over my shoulder to see David Tøllin smiling at me. He has the look of a hunter who's about to take a sure shot. His eyes seem to look right into the marrow of my bones.

"And how's the sexiest man at this party?" he grins.

I say nothing. I stare into those eyes of his. My heart is racing. "I could eat you alive," he says with a low wolven growl. The heat in my body begins to rise. I feel like a fly trapped on a spider's web waiting for my inevitable demise.

"Take a pill, tiger," Howard scolds David. "Release thy grip on this handsome knight." David laughs and withdraws from me.

"So how have you been enjoying Calgary so far?" He asks, his eyes still penetrating me.

"Well, ever since I arrived I think I may have slept about three or four hours. I've seen quite a bit, and met so many people that everything so far seems like a blur."

"You'll find Calgarians are really friendly," says David.

"Some of them are more friendly than others," says Howard.

David laughs. He hands me a business card and says, "Don't lose this."

I look at the card. *Vastervik Imports*, it says, *Fine Scandinavian Furniture, David Tollin President.*

"Oh, you're in the import biz are you?" I say.

"Come and see me when you want to buy some furniture," David says, "in fact, come and see me even if you don't want to buy any furniture. My home phone number is on the back."

I turn the card over, and sure enough there it is.

"I'll talk to you a little later," David says as he kisses me. Then he looks at Howard and bows, "Your Highness."

"Guards, remove this creature from my presence," Howard answers without smiling. I watch as David laughs and disappears back into the tidal swell of the crowd. I don't know what it is, but I feel like helpless prey when I'm around him, and somehow I find that feeling irresistible. In my mind, just for an instant, I can see David and me in bed together, our naked bodies thrashing from one side to the other. I can almost feel his tongue probing my mouth, and I feel myself getting hard.

"Watch him," Howard cautions interrupting my fantasy.

"What?" I say emerging from my daze.

"Watch him," Howard cautions once more wagging his finger at me. "I like David, he's a nice guy, and I've known him for years. But he's busy."

I look at the card; I look back at the direction David went. I put his card in my shirt pocket. I look at Howard, smile, and for the first time in my life, I hear myself say, "Maybe it's time that I lived a little."

"Remember that old saying about playing with fire," Howard says to me with a knowing smile.

"Here you go," says Marcel handing my glass to me, "did I miss anything?"

"No," says Howard. "Sir Lancelot and I were just having a scintillating conversation about how busy some people can be." Then he turns his attention back to the food table.

Marcel gives me a puzzled look. I glance back at the direction David went and put my hand over the shirt pocket his card is in.

∞

A knock comes to my door, then another, and another. "All right, already, all right," I mumble as I roll out of bed, put on my housecoat, and open the door of my room. Before me stands a handsome clean-shaven young man with sandy blond hair. His wide-eyed innocent look accentuates his apologetic smile as he asks, "Sorry to bother you, but are you Bryn Menzies?"

In my half-dazed state I mumble, "yes."

"There's a phone call for you," he says pointing at the phone in the hallway, the receiver resting on the small wooden shelf below it.

"Oh," I shake my head, "Thank you." I stumble over to the phone and pick up the receiver.

"Hello."

"So do you want to buy any furniture?"

"Uh, David?"

"Yep." The sound of his voice makes my heart skip a beat in excitement. "How did you know how to find me?"

I watch the young man who knocked on my door turn and walk down the hall, glancing back at me and smiling with every few steps.

"You were surprisingly easy to find," David says. "I just phoned the switchboard, told them that I wanted to get hold of Lieutenant

Bryn Menzies and next thing, here you are. I thought there would be a little more security than that, being a military base."

My heart picks up its pace, "To what do I owe the pleasure of this phone call?"

"Do you and Marcel have plans today?"

"No, I told Marcel I wanted to be on my own today, to rest."

"Good. Can I talk you into brunch?"

"Maybe."

"Since that's a qualified yes, I'll take as a definite yes."

"I don't seem to have a choice."

"No."

I laugh, "Okay, when do you want to get together?"

"Meet me at 11 at my store. You still have my card don't you?"

"Yeah, I do. But I still don't know how to get there."

David waits till I go into my room to get a paper and pen to write the instructions how to get to his store. When I return, he gives me directions and we confirm the time we'll meet. I return to my room, throw my housecoat across the bed, grab my shaving gear and soap, take my bath towel, wrap it around my waist, and head to the showers.

As I approach the washroom, I can hear the sound of a solitary shower running. I enter, walk past a row of cubicles to my right, and sinks with small mirrors on the wall to my left. In front of me, a solitary wooden bench is spread across the width of the room, and to the left side of it, the showers. I can smell the faint sweet scent of shampoo as I throw my towel over a hook and enter.

The young guy who knocked on my door only a few minutes ago is the only person in here besides me. He looks at me and gives me a sweet smile, making him look more boyish than he already does.

"Hi," he says.

"Hi," I smile back.

"I'm Jim Whitelaw."

"I'm Bryn, but you know that already."

Jim laughs. "I knew you had to be Bryn Menzies."

"How?"

"Because you're the only new guy whose moved into this wing of the barrack block so far this summer."

"Lucky me."

"Where are you in from?" Jim asks.

"Borden, and you?"

"I got here a year ago from Suffield."

"Lucky you," I say as I turn the shower on and adjust the temperature. I move underneath the torrent of water and let the warmth of its millions of tongues run down my body. I close my eyes and turn my back to it. I tilt my head forward and let the rushing water massage the back of my neck. I raise my head slowly and open my eyes to see Jim quickly turn his head away from me.

I watch him from the corner of my eye and he seems to fumble as if he doesn't know what to do next. Then he moves his face under his shower, tilts his head back, and opens his mouth to fill it with water. I watch intently as after a few seconds he slowly spits the water out of his mouth and lets it run down his chin, his neck and his chest.

I watch the water as it runs down to his cock. I look at his cock, its length, its girth. I stare at its pink head, the patch of dark hair that surrounds it, and his balls that hang beneath it all. I wonder what his cock looks like when it's hard. I wonder what his balls taste like. My eyes travel back up his washboard stomach and his well-developed chest, then his smiling eyes meet mine. This jolts me back to reality like a slap across the face. I'm totally embarrassed.

"Sorry," I apologize to Jim.

"That's okay," he smiles and assures me.

I quickly soap down, wash my hair, rinse off and want nothing more than to get out of here as fast as I can. I turn off the shower, retrieve my towel from its hook and beat a hasty retreat to my room. I sit on my bed still dripping wet and find I have to catch my breath. It's bad enough that Jim caught me looking at him, but when our eyes met, that just struck a little too close to home for me. Not here in the barracks, I think, not now, not when I haven't even started work here.

I get up and slowly dry myself. After everything that's gone on in the past couple of days, and the fun I've had with Marcel I suddenly feel as if I've betrayed myself. How can I turn on my heels and run from all of this again? I guess I still fear this gay thing after all.

I'm startled by a knock on my door. I open it to see Jim with his towel wrapped around him.

"Was it something I said?" he asks.

"What do you mean?"

"You beat such a hasty retreat from the showers I was wondering if I said or did something to put you off."

"No, no, it wasn't anything you did."

"Can I come in?"

"Well, I'm just getting ready to visit a buddy of mine soon," then I look at his boyish smile and let him in. I close the door.

"Look," I say, "I apologize for what happened there."

"What are you talking about?"

"You know, in the showers. I guess I was, you know, looking at you."

Jim shrugs his shoulders and says, "Nothing happened."

"Still, sorry about that."

"It sounds like you feel more uncomfortable about it than I do. No problem, don't worry about it. I just want to know if I could buy you a drink sometime. You know, a kind of welcome to Calgary drink."

"Yeah, that would be good."

"I know a great place away from the base we could go to, if that's okay with you?"

"I'd like that."

"Okay," says Jim smiling, "let's make it sometime soon."

"Yeah," I smile back at him, "sometime soon."

There's a bit of a sweet tension in the air as the two of us stand here silently looking at each other with smiles plastered across our mouths.

"Well," says Jim, "I, uh, better let you," his hands make motions at me, "get ready I guess."

"Yeah, I guess I should get ready if I'm going to be there on time."

Jim reaches behind him for the doorknob, "Well, we're on for drinks then?"

"Definitely."

Jim opens the door and just as he turns toward it, it hits him right in his face.

"Whoa, are you okay Jim?"

He just holds his hand over his mouth and nose, nods his head, waves at me, and leaves closing the door behind him.

I smile then chuckle at what just happened.

∞

I arrive at the front of David's store and I look at the displays in the windows. Pieces of blond teakwood furniture accent leather couches, and tall cacti are interspersed throughout the scene. The windows themselves have writing along the sides of them that say "Living Space." The door opens, and there's David with that hungry spider smile again. He motions me to come inside. Our eyes are locked on each other as I smile and step by him in the doorway without saying a word.

"Welcome to my world," he says, and as I focus my attention on the right-hand wall full of crystal decanters, I hear the door lock behind me.

"This is a nice place," I say, surveying the showroom.

"Thanks, it pays the mortgage. I've got a private stash of wines in my office, why don't we have a drink, while I show you around, then we can go."

"At eleven o'clock in the morning?"

"Why not? We were going to be having champagne and orange juice with brunch, so what's the big deal."

I grin and shrug my shoulders, "Well alright then."

"Follow me."

As we make our way to the back of the store I ask, "How did you get into this business anyway?"

"I took a cue from my father who was in the import business in Sweden. That's how he and my mother met. She was on a buying trip with my grandfather to Sweden, and my father happened to live in the same town where they were staying. They met, started a long distance love affair, and eventually he came to Canada and they were married."

"Was your dad from Stockholm?"

"No, Vastervik."

"Ah, that explains the name of the business."

David smiles and nods as he opens a pair of swinging doors that lead into the back. I step through and look at the disarray that suddenly surrounds me. This almost-chaos is in total contrast to the orderly appearance of the showroom. Ceiling to floor shelving units span the right-hand wall, with the bigger boxes stacked neatly along the bottom and gradually get smaller the higher the stacking goes.

"Do you like white or red?" David asks.

"Red, thanks."

David disappears into a small office. Meanwhile I look over to the left-hand wall where rolls of material stand upright in a corner and are in various stages of unravel. A stack of folded boxes sits in front of them. A heavy wooden work table sprawls across the length of the room and is piled high with packing tape, pieces of cut cloth, small pieces of Styrofoam packing "popcorn," scissors and x-acto knives, while a couple of upright dollies for transporting boxes stand by its side.

"This is the nerve centre of the whole operation," David says as he rests two glasses of wine on the table and smiles proudly with his arms outstretched on either side of him. "We unpack our imports for display on the floor, and we pack things for delivery to your door."

"I hope that's not your slogan," I say.

David laughs, "Stinks, doesn't it?"

"Pee-yew," I reply.

He laughs a hearty belly laugh, picks up the glasses and comes over to me. He hands me a glass and says, "Welcome to Calgary."

"Thanks," I say as we clink our glasses and take a sip. Our eyes don't leave each other as we drink. He takes my glass from me and rests both on the table. He wraps his arms around me and we kiss. He stands back a step and stares directly into my eyes. His face shows no emotion. We're silent.

He goes over to one of the shelving units, moves a large piece of plywood to reveal a large, mattress-sized piece of foam. He pushes it over and it falls with barely a sound to the floor. His back still to me he unbuttons and removes his shirt. He turns to me, his face still showing no emotion. I can feel the hair on the back of my neck stand on end as I look into his eyes. I feel like I'm dinner once again, and he's coming toward me with a knife, fork and a hungry look.

He wraps one arm around my waist and with the other he holds the back of my head, his lips planted firmly on mine. I wrap my arms around him like a willing meal. We press our lips together and our kissing gets deeper as I feel my crotch getting harder. David unbuttons my shirt pushing the cloth aside and slowly moving both his hands across my bare chest. He moves his face to my chest and licks my nipple. Pleasure rushes through me and my body feels liquid as he raises his face and we kiss once more.

I feel him reach for my belt buckle and undo it without fumbling. He rubs and squeezes my crotch then says, "We'll eat, and then we'll go for brunch."

∞

I'm laying naked on the piece of foam with David. He has one arm around me and is snoozing. All is quiet except for the hum of a fan from somewhere in the room. I feel spent. I look upward and my eyes follow the pipes that twist like strands of spaghetti along the high ceiling. Industrial lighting fixtures hang down from above us like long, thick metallic hoods. They cast a strong harsh glare on us like we are on a movie set, and just for an instant I feel like I've been in a porn movie.

I glance to my side to see our clothes in two small heaps by the table and then scattered toward the place where we're laying. Further across the concrete floor a big brown spider casually strolls from underneath one of the shelving units toward the table. It pauses briefly and seems to turn to look at us lying on the foam. Then it quickly disappears to the safety of the dark underneath the table. My eyes travel up to the top of the table where our glasses of red wine still rest.

David's hand moves from its resting spot up to my nipple. He gives it a gentle tug, he moves himself around to kiss me again.

"You hungry," he asks.

"Yeah."

"Good. Let's go for something to eat."

We slowly get up, get dressed, and walk down to the restaurant, which David says is only a few blocks away.

It's almost one in the afternoon as we head north along Fourth Avenue South West. The main streets are quiet, as all the stores are closed for Sunday. There's a small crowd gathered on the front steps of a small church we pass. An old man and the minister look like they're having a frank discussion while an older woman in a blue flowered dress and white hat bids us good day as we pass.

We are about to pass the nightclub that I was at on Friday night, when David says, "We're here."

I look at him in disbelief, "but this is a gay bar isn't it?"

"Gay disco by night and restaurant during the day," he says as he opens the door for me. Then he laughs, "Are you going to stand there all day with your mouth open, or are you coming inside?"

I say nothing and go inside. A good-looking young woman greets us. "Just sit anywhere guys," she smiles. David leads me to a table near the dance floor, while Billie Holiday sings a song over the sound system.

"Champagne and orange juice," David asks.

"Sounds good to me," I answer.

I see David look up and over my shoulder just as I feel a hand rest on it. I look around to have my heart leap to my throat. It's Jim, that guy in the shower from my barrack block.

"I thought that was you I saw coming in," he says.

"Ah...," is all I can muster.

"Who's your cute friend, Bryn?" David asks.

I hesitate.

"I'm Jim," he says reaching over me to shake hands with David.

"I'm David," he says with that hungry look.

"Have you guys known each other very long?"

"No," says David, "we met the other night."

Then Jim puts his hand on the back of my head. "It'll be great having another member of the clan in the same barracks. We'll have some great times together."

"Hey Jim, ya comin' or what," says one of the guys in the small group waiting for him by the front door.

"I've got to go. Nice to meet you David."

"Nice meeting you too," David says as he hands Jim one of his business cards. Jim looks at it.

"So you own Vastervik Imports, I like the furniture in your shop."

"Well come by sometime and I'll give you a private tour of the place," David says with a wink.

"I'll do that," Jim smiles back. "I'm so glad I've run into you here this afternoon Bryn. You and I have a lot to talk about. See you." Jim turns and joins his friends and they exit the restaurant.

"He seems like a really nice guy, and he's cute too," David says. I am at a loss for words.

∞

The four of them look at me silently. "I don't believe you," one of my sisters says. "You're in the military, and you've had lots of girlfriends."

"It was that fuckin' Neil, wasn't it?" one of my brothers-in-law spits. "What did he do to you on your way out west?"

"He didn't do anything that I didn't let him do," I respond. Stunned silence.

"Bryn," says my other brother-in-law, "we told you that it wasn't a good idea to take that faggot with you out west. We—"

"We told you the only way to handle guys like him," my first brother-in-law interrupts. "Why the hell didn't you just beat the shit out of him and leave him in a ditch like we said?"

"Will you guys stop it," my oldest sister says. Then she looks at me and says in a quiet voice. "Bryn, this may be your idea of a joke, but it isn't funny."

"Sis, I'm not joking," I say.

She sighs an exasperated sigh, "Can you imagine what this will do to Mom and Dad? This could very well give Dad a heart attack. Do you want to be responsible for that?"

"I never did trust that Neil guy," my other sister says. "Look at what a fool he's made of you."

"Will you give me credit for making up my own mind? Yes, I've had lots of girlfriends, and yes, I'm in the military, but dammit, I like guys! Furthermore I like liking guys!"

The air in the room is thick as the four of them sit in stunned silence once more. That's when my oldest brother-in-law gets up, comes over to me, and punches me in the mouth.

This startles me awake. I immediately brush my hand over my mouth, and breathe a sigh of relief as I realize it was only a dream. I glance around me and listen to the silence of my room. I look out the window to see the light of the street lamps shining on thick snowflakes as they fall. I look beside me to see the back of Jim's head poking out of a heap of flannel sheets and a comforter. Then I look at my clock radio: 5:00 am, and it's Saturday. I get up, put on my housecoat and go into the kitchen for a glass of water. As I turn on the tap, I think of the dream and remind myself that it is my life, and whatever happens, my decisions are mine.

After all, these have probably been some of the best months of my entire life. At the end of July, with Marcel's help, I found this apartment. It sure beats life in the barracks, and it seems easier for me to keep my work and private life separate. At this point in time that means a lot to me. I like my place. It's the spot where I feel totally free.

I now live in an area of town called The Beltline. It's just south of the downtown core. There are very few single family homes in the area, mainly apartment buildings, both high-rise and three to four-storey walk-ups. Marcel says it's the gay area of town, and from what I've seen in the last few months, I can say it's true.

Like the weekend I moved in here; I went out to get some groceries at the local Safeway, and while I was there, I saw guys cruising guys everywhere I turned. I couldn't believe what I was seeing. I mean it was so blatant, I was shocked but intrigued. I told Marcel about it on the phone when I got home, and he said that particular Safeway is notorious for that kind of blatant cruising, especially on Saturday mornings.

I go into the living room and pull back the curtain on my balcony door to the fresh blanket of white. For a normally busy area of the city, all is quiet. I look to the rooftops of the surrounding buildings to see plumes of white smoke slowly rising from every chimney assuring warmth to all who sleep. The branches of the evergreens that line this street appear to be weighed down with thick white cotton, as they bend toward the sidewalks. On the street three floors below me, the snow covering the road is undisturbed by any trace of a vehicle.

A solitary figure trudges slowly down the sidewalk, ankle deep in the snow. It's hard to tell if it is a man or woman because he or she is bundled up and completely covered. I can see this person's breath from their scarf-covered nose and mouth as they walk bravely into the onslaught of thick flakes on this first snowfall of the year. The falling snow quickly covers the trail of footprints. I watch as the figure trudges to an apartment building two-doors down and across the street from my perch. He or she approaches the door, stamps their feet to shake off excess snow, fumbles for their key, and unlocks the front door. Instantly the figure is inside the warmth and shelter of that building.

A lot has changed in my life just in the last few months. I feel much more at ease with this gay thing, and I mean that big time. I know my sisters wouldn't approve and I'm still very nervous about telling them. I think about that nightmare again. Well, maybe I'll tell them about my new life some day, but then again maybe I won't. Although, as I say, I'm still careful to keep my private life separate from my career. I could be discharged or worse yet, Court-martialled. Then I don't know what I would do. But I feel like a new door has opened for me, and I want to explore what this life has to offer.

For example, in October Marcel, Jim, and I went to see Craig Russell at the Jubilee Auditorium. He was the star of the movie Outrageous in 1977. I went to see it one weekend while I was still at R.M.C. in Kingston. I was impressed by his many imitations of big name female stars. I never thought I would be seeing him live with an auditorium with so many "out" gay people.

I smile as I think of that concert again. The capacity audience seemed to be a diverse crowd of straight and gay people dressed in everything from formal jackets and ties, to jeans and sports jackets, to full drag to full leather.

I remember the show opening with an empty stage and Craig's voice singing over the microphone, (a la Aretha Franklin), *You Make Me Feel Like A Natural...Person.* The audience erupted into laughter with Craig saying, "Gotcha!"

From this point we were treated to almost two hours of hilarity from Craig's impersonations of: Barbra Streisand, Bette Midler, Janis Joplin, Bette Davis, Carol Channing, Mae West and Peggy Lee among others.

There were two highlights of the concert for me. One was a very poignant performance he did of Judy Garland. He played what she may have been like during her drug addled final days. He played her being lonely and confused where she hung on to her triumphs from her Carnegie Hall concert, to Dorothy in the Wizard of Oz.

Then there was his impersonation of Anita Bryant to which everyone—especially the gay kids—roared with laughter. The conductor of the small orchestra directed the musicians to hit every sour note they possibly could while Craig/Anita sang *Battle Hymn of the Republic.* Every once in a while Craig would stop singing the song and say, "I'm not getting any support around here!" To those of us present, it was an obvious reference to her anti-gay tour of Canada last year; which had to be cancelled due to poor attendance at the various venues.

I chuckle as I fondly recall that evening. I remember feeling a little chauvinistic when I left the auditorium. *Yeah,* I thought, *we gays are a pretty talented bunch.* Then I stopped when I realized what I had thought and I haven't looked back.

After all these months I'm thinking of Neil again. I wonder what life would have been like if I hadn't left him in Winnipeg. Would the two of us be living in a place like this? I wonder what he's up to now. Did he stay in Winnipeg with his friends? Did he move to Toronto like he always wanted to do? I guess the biggest regret of my life will be how I treated him.

I'm momentarily distracted by the sound of Jim coughing in the bedroom. He stopped smoking a couple of weeks ago, and it's still driving him nuts. Now if only Marcel would quit smoking—not bloody likely; he's stubborn that way.

Jim and I met for that drink he wanted to take me out for at The Parkside Continental, much to my initial hesitation. In the short time that followed, while Jim and I were getting to know each other, Marcel and I found this apartment for me. When I moved out of the barracks, Jim started coming over for visits quite often, that's when we got to know each other a lot better.

He's a real sweetheart. Born in Thunder Bay and raised in rural Manitoba, he looks like the wide-eyed innocent country boy gone to the big city. He's cute, he's clumsy, and it seems all of the gay guys want to bed him.

He does have some quirky little habits, though. He likes to carry around a small notepad and pen, and every once in a while I'll catch him scribbling something down on it. Finally one day I asked him.

"What are you doing?"

"Oh just writing something."

"What are you writing?"

He shrugged his shoulders, "Oh, just some things."

"Like..." I said, prompting him.

He smiled an embarrassed smile and said, "Just some of my thoughts and feelings about things."

"Things?"

"Well, I've been reading this book called Notes to Myself—"

"I've heard of it—"

"Hugh Prather put his thoughts, feelings, and impressions about various things on paper. I thought it was an interesting idea, so I began to do it, that's all."

"So what are your thoughts and impressions right now?" He smiled at me again and said, "You're not going to let this go are you?"

I shook my head, awaiting an answer.

"Okay, okay " he said giving in to my curiosity. *'#57- Bryn and I went to see that movie Alien last night. I liked it, except for that part where the alien pops out of John Hurt's stomach. But it was a good film other than that. I like being with Bryn, I feel I can tell him anything, and he'll take it all in stride. I feel like he won't judge me."*

A smile draws across my lips. That was one of the nicest thoughts anybody's ever had about me. It's a thought I feel totally unworthy of, especially when I think about the way I treated Neil.

I look out the window once more. As I recall it was about that time we began going to bed together. That was when I found out about Jim's other quirks. He isn't the wide-eyed innocent country boy that he appears to be. In fact, he's introduced me to things I would never have thought about only six months ago.

He likes to take Polaroids sometimes when he, Marcel, and I are in bed together. I told him that as long as he keeps them hidden away, I don't mind. Here I am, a kinky officer in the military. It's Jim's favourite sex game; Marcel really gets into it, and I love to play it as well. You see, that's the third quirky thing that's happened, the three of us have become lovers together.

I never thought I would be involved in a threesome-type relationship, especially a kinky one, but this just clicked. Howard has started calling us the Holy Trinity. What's more it seems others are beginning to follow suit. It makes me chuckle. It's like an acknowledgement that people accept our type of relationship even if they don't understand it. It's too bad Marcel has company in from Red Deer this weekend, for Jim and I sure notice his absence.

We all still have our separate homes, Jim still lives in the barracks, Marcel and Vince still share their house, and I live here, but every weekend when the three of us can, we gather at my place and spend our time together and share a bed. Just last month the three of us pitched in to buy a king-sized bed from David's shop so there would be more room for us at night. There's only enough room in the bedroom to accommodate the bed, a night table and dresser. I'm not exactly sure how it was that Jim, Marcel and I got into a relationship like this. As I'm thinking about it, I believe it was late

September. It was a Sunday afternoon, and the three of us were over here for a couple of drinks.

We were going to go to an early evening showing of the new movie La Cage Aux Folles. I had gone into the kitchen to pour another Scotch, and when I returned to the living room, Marcel and Jim were on the couch, their arms around each other and their lips pressed together in a deep kiss. I was neither shocked nor surprised. Sitting in a chair facing the couch, I put my Scotch on the coffee table and watched them.

Marcel turned his attention my way and beckoned me closer. I came over to the couch, and Marcel gave me a deep kiss, then Jim joined in. I guess that's where it started. And I haven't regretted a single moment the three of us have been together.

I look out once more to the falling snow and think about the first night the three of us got into anything I would consider kinky.

We have a small black leather bag full of sex toys like handcuffs, tit clamps, a couple of paddles and other accessories, which we keep in the top drawer of the dresser. I have to admit I wasn't sure about venturing into this territory, but Jim's encouragement—*C'mon, be adventurous. At least then you can say you tried it and didn't like it*—won me over.

I continue to look at the falling snow, I hear a stirring in the bedroom, and then shuffling into the hallway. The bathroom light flips on followed by the loud report of the toilet seat slamming down.

"Shit!" I hear Jim swear in a low voice. That's followed by the sound of the toilet seat being lifted once more and the sound of a guy having a leak.

I look out the window once again, and I'm reminded that Christmas is a little more than a month away. I'll be heading back to Christmas in Oshawa, then I'll be back here for New Years. I'd like to bring in the new decade with the two guys I feel closest to.

The toilet flushes. Jim comes into the living room where the only light is coming from the street lamp through the narrow part in the curtains. He wraps his arms around me. I undo my housecoat and open it for him. "Brrr, it's cold," Jim says as he presses his body against mine. I laugh as I wrap the housecoat around the two of us as much as it will go. We kiss and look out of the parted curtain to the cold prairie winter night.

∞

Happy New Year! It's goodbye 1970s; the year 1980 will be here in only a few hours. The radio has been playing *We Don't talk Anymore* by Cliff Richard as Jim and I are in my idling car waiting for Marcel to finish work. He works at a restaurant here at the Chinook Mall, and the southern city limits lie only a few minute's drive down MacLeod Trail from here.

We're picking Marcel up and then heading south to Lethbridge where there's a big New Years Party set to happen. I'm looking forward to it, although I notice that Jim has been unusually quiet this evening. Just to get him talking I ask,

"Did you say these people having the party are friends of David's?"

"No, they're friends of Honker's and Mark's, but I imagine that David is driving down with them because Lethbridge is new territory to hunt."

I laugh because that is exactly the reason David would even consider going on a trip like this. As we listen to the radio, I look around this slush-covered parking lot at the flurry of people heading home getting ready for the coming night of partying. Christmas lights twinkle at us from the outside of the building. A steady line of vehicles pull up; collect waiting passengers, then they drive away.

Then the familiar opening chords of a song begin.

"I like this song," I say as I quickly reach over to the radio and turn up the volume. Even though it's an old MoTown song, I like the originality in the way it's presented as the lead singer, who sounds just like Queen Elizabeth, recites:

"The best things in life are free, but you can give them to the birds and the bees. I want money. That's what I want."

I recite the lyrics while the song is playing, and I notice that Jim seems a little more withdrawn. He undoes his jacket and takes his notepad from his shirt pocket. He scribbles something furiously on the paper. I know him well enough that when he does something like this, then something's really bothering him.

So I turn down the music and ask, "Jim, what's the matter? Ever since I picked you up at the barracks tonight something's been on your mind."

Jim stops writing, glances out the passenger window then sighs,

"Some of the guys in the barracks have clued into the fact that I'm gay."

Time seems to come to a sudden shrieking halt.

"What makes you think they know?" I ask.

Jim fumbles through his pants pockets looking for something. "I found this under my door this morning," he says taking a small piece of crumpled blue paper out of one of his pockets and handing it to me.

I unravel it and read it. It says, *Happy New Year Cocksucker!*

I stare at it silently. Then I read it again just to make sure I believe what I'm reading. I can see the paper trembling in my hands, and I can feel a knot in my gut. I slowly raise my head and stare out the window.

"Well, maybe this is a joke," I say, not quite believing what I'm saying.

"I don't think so," says Jim, "you know Bob Harrington and Mike Sloan?"

"Yeah."

"Well, for the last couple of weeks I can see them passing comments back and forth to each other, then they look at me and start laughing."

"That doesn't necessarily mean they know you're gay. It could be anything. This could all be some stupid prank," I tell myself as much as I'm telling Jim.

Jim shrugs, "I can't help but feel like I'm marked. Especially when they make it obvious that they are referring to me when they do these things."

"Do you think it's them that left this note?"

"I don't know."

"As I say, maybe it's just a stupid prank."

"Well, I wish I could believe that," Jim says, "because yesterday while I was at the mess having dinner, Sloan yells over to me... hey Whitelaw, and when I turned around to look at him, and he blew me a kiss from across the room. The group of guys he was with, who were all watching me, laughed then turned their backs to me. Sloan said something to them and they all laughed again while some of them looked over at me for a second time. Then this piece of paper appears under my door this morning."

I'm feeling physically sick all of a sudden. I glance over to the mall just on time to see Marcel at the main entrance. He quickly glances around, spots the car, and hurries over to the two of us waiting inside. I look at the crumpled piece of paper in my hands. The last thing I feel like doing is going to a party now. With a big smile on his face Marcel opens the passenger door.

"You guys ready for the Eighties?" he chirps.

We look at him with glum expressions. He looks at Jim, then me, then back at Jim.

"You guys can't feel *that* bad about saying goodbye to platforms shoes can you?"

A smile draws across Jim's face as he turns and looks at me.

"Marcel do you feel like driving?" I ask.

"Sure," he says.

"Since you know how to get there anyway " I add.

I get out of the car and into the back seat, while Marcel comes around and takes his place behind the wheel. We pull out of the parking lot and turn south onto MacLeod Trail.

∞

I haven't said much since we've been on the road. Jim has explained everything to Marcel and the two of them have talked a lot about it since. I've been slouched quietly here in the back seat with my arms crossed over my chest staring at the passing scenery. There hasn't been a lot to see except the vast expanse of dark, over the flatness of Southern Alberta.

Occasionally I've seen the passing glimpses of humanity, especially when approaching smaller farming towns. Names like: Bobcat, John Deere, Alberta Wheat Pool, Co-Op, and Husky Truck Stops all illuminate—if only briefly—the darkness. Once through the towns though, I've seen only the occasional light of a farmhouse, off the highway in the distance.

"Are you still with us, Bryn?" Marcel says as he looks at me through the rear-view mirror.

"Yeah, I guess I am," I say as I move forward and lean against the front seats.

"So what do you guys think about all this?" Marcel asks his eyes not leaving the road. Jim and I look at each other.

"I mean," Marcel continues, "if this thing affects one of us, it's bound to affect all of us."

"Well that's true," I say.

Jim grins, "Any brilliant suggestions, Marcel?"

"Not right now," he answers.

"Well," I say, "this whole thing makes me nervous because this is no joke."

"No," says Marcel, "nobody's joking over this one."

"What changed your mind?" asks Jim looking at me.

"What do you mean?"

"When we were waiting for Marcel you were convinced this was a prank."

"I actually said that maybe it was. But now having given it some thought, maybe you should just move out of the barracks Jim."

"Don't be too hasty to run," Marcel cautions, "Okay, we agree that this is no joke, but aren't you working with these guys anyway? The last thing you need right now is to give them more ammo against you."

"I'm not sure that I follow," says Jim.

"They might look upon you moving out of the barracks as being a coward. Then what happens when you have to face these guys at work each day?" Jim shrugs his shoulders. "I honestly don't know, Marcel. I wish I could answer those questions."

The music on the radio has faded the further south from Calgary we've gone. At this point it cross fades between the barely-audible Calgary station we were listening to and static. Jim fiddles with the tuning dial and settles on a corny country station out of Medicine Hat. Ronnie Milsap is trying his hand at the disco craze, now that it's dying. He's singing, *Get It Up To Get Down.* A Country singer playing disco on a country station in Southern Alberta, for the first time on this trip I feel a smile on my lips as I think about that irony. I shake my head and chuckle.

"All I can say about the situation at hand," says Marcel, "is that it's New Years Eve. There's really nothing we can do about it right now, so let's enjoy tonight, and we can tackle this thing when we get back to Calgary."

"I guess that makes sense," Jim says.

"Remember," says Marcel smiling at us, "we're all in this together, and that's not such a scary thing."

Then he extends his right hand toward Jim and says, "Give me your right hand Jim."

Jim puts his right hand over Marcel's.

"Now you Bryn," Marcel says turning to me.

I follow suit by putting my right hand over Jim's hand.

"We're all in this together," declares Marcel, "ain't nothin' we can't tackle."

"Amen to that," says Jim with a huge smile on his face.

"There's Lethbridge now," says Marcel, breaking our clasp and pointing ahead of us

In the distance I can see a carpet of blue streetlights spread along the horizon. I've noticed that about prairie cities, the streetlights seem to have a blue glow, as opposed to the yellow/orange glow of the streetlights of Ontario towns.

It isn't long before a sign with an arrow pointing straight ahead directs us to Lethbridge City Centre via 13th Street North. Before I know it, we've entered the city. Now it's like a blur. Straight down 13th Street then we hang a left on 10th Avenue South to what looks like a hospital. That's when we hang a right and snake our way down a couple of side streets. Marcel finds a parking spot and stops the engine.

"Here we are," he says. He points to a grey stucco bungalow across the street from us that's trimmed with multi-coloured Christmas lights. I watch as two guys approach the illuminated front door and are stopped by a short, stocky guy with a moustache. They talk for a moment, then the couple turn and walk down the side of the house toward the back.

We get out of the car. I grab my bottle of Scotch, and Jim and I follow Marcel across the street toward the house. The stocky man at the door grins at us as we approach, then his grin turns to delight as he recognizes Marcel.

"Marcel!" he exclaims as he bounds out the door and gives him a bear hug.

"I haven't seen you for a couple of years! How have things been!"

"They've been really good," he says. Then he addresses Jim and I, "this is Morris."

"And these must be the other two-thirds of The Holy Trinity," a smiling Morris says to us.

Jim and I look at each other and grin.

Marcel rolls his eyes, "David must be here already," he says.

"Oh yes," Morris says, "he arrived a couple of hours ago with Mark and Honker. I have to say, that guy is busy."

"What's he done?" Marcel asks with a knowing smile.

"Well it seems he's rounded up a few guys to go somewhere later for some kind of a New Years group-grope thing," Morris answers.

"It figures," I chuckle.

"He's probably trying to recruit more as we speak," says Jim.

"This is Jim," Marcel says to Morris.

"And you must be Bryn," Morris says to me while shaking Jim's hand.

"Yours Truly," I reply. We shake hands. Another small cluster of people are coming up the driveway.

"Well listen," says Morris, "we'll talk later. Why don't you guys go inside. I'm asking everyone to use the back door, because the party is in the basement."

"Okay, we'll talk later," says Marcel.

"Nice to meet you," Jim says.

"Likewise," says Morris smiling back.

We leave Morris at his sentry and walk silently down the side of the house, following the sound of the disco music from the back door. I think about that note under Jim's door this morning. Marcel's words from earlier this evening come to mind once more—let's just enjoy tonight and we can tackle this thing when we get back to Calgary. But a cold rush makes me shiver a little as I think about what might lie ahead for 1980.

∞

It's a cold, dark January afternoon as Jim and I walk down the corridor toward his room on the second floor of the barracks. I can hear the music of Blondie coming from one of the rooms at the far end of the hall, "*When I met you in the restaurant, you could tell I was no debutante....*"

On the way I catch a glimpse of the private lives of some of the officers who live here because their doors are left open. The room we just passed to my left had framed black and white photos neatly arranged in a straight line across a small wall between two windows. While a room further down to my right had a poster-sized picture of a beach hanging on the wall with Summerside P.E.I. written in script across the top of it.

We reach Jim's room. He takes his keys from his pocket and drops them on the floor making a ka-chink sound that slightly reverberates down the hall. From the corner of my eye, I can see a figure appear in one of the open doorways two rooms away. It's Harrington. He leans against the side of his doorway and folds his arms with a smile on his face that says, A-ha!

He looks into his room and motions with his head as if telling somebody to come here. Sloan peeks his head into the hall, and gives me a broad smile that says, I knew it!

"Shit," Jim says as he retrieves the keys then unlocks the door. I look firmly at Harrington and Sloan and say, "You guys got a problem?"

Sloan looks at Harrington, smiles, and disappears back into the room. Harrington gives me a *fuck-you* chuckle, slithers back inside and shuts the door.

We enter Jim's room and I close the door behind me.

"Those guys are really getting on my nerves," Jim says as he goes over to his closet, "Everywhere I go on Base they seem to be there. Everything I do at work or here at the barracks, they're there."

He takes out a weekend bag and throws it on his bed with a disgusted look on his face.

"It's almost like they're keeping close tabs on me or some-thing." His unzips the bag, throws open the flap and starts packing some things.

"Then it's a good thing you're coming with me," I say.

He's going to spend a few days with Marcel and I at the apart-ment. We've agreed we can better discuss things if the three of us are together and can figure out what to do about this whole episode with Sloan and Harrington.

I stand near the door with my hands in my pockets looking around Jim's room. I quickly wipe some dust off the top of his chest of drawers. The walls are full of photographs that he has taken over the years that are enlarged and framed. The one I like best of a mother with three boys around her. One looks like he's about sixteen or seventeen years old, and the other two appear to be about twelve or thirteen. In the background is the U.S. Pavilion at Expo '67 in Montreal.

One of the younger boys stands close to the woman's side and has a shy smile on his face.

"I always wanted to ask," I say to Jim pointing at the young boy, "Is that you?"

Jim stops what he's doing, comes over beside me, and looks at the photo and smiles. "Yeah, that's me when I was twelve years old. My father took that picture when we were at Expo '67. It's my all time favourite because it's one of the only photos of me with my mom."

I know that his mother died of cancer about the time that he was 16 years old. He stares at the photo with a sad and silent smile. I put my arm around him and he rests his head on my shoulder.

"You were close to your mom weren't you?"

"Yeah," he says not lifting his head, "we could talk and joke about anything for hours." Then he says in a low voice, "She knew I was gay even before I did."

"How do you know that?"

"She asked me one day when I was 14 if I liked guys instead of girls."

"What did you say?"

"I said I didn't know."

"What did she say then?"

"She hugged me and told me that it was perfectly alright if it turned out I did like guys. I remember she smiled and said, 'Honey, if you do like guys a lot of people are not going to like you because of it. Don't listen to a word they say to you, and never let anybody tell you they're better than you are.' I try not to forget those words. Although sometimes it's hard—like now."

I stroke the back of his head. "And who's this kid?" I ask pointing to the second of the younger boys.

"He was my closest friend Cliff. He came along with us at the last minute."

"What do you mean *was* your closest friend?"

"I haven't seen him in a few years. Then again, I haven't been back home for a few years. We silently look at the photo for a few moments more. I break our silence.

"I'll help you pack and we can get out of here," I whisper.

"Sure," he says flashing that boyish grin at me.

Jim puts his shaving gear together while I go to one of his drawers and pull out shirts, underwear and socks. I put everything neatly on the bed for Jim to pack.

"Hey," he chuckles, "I'm only going to your place for a few days, not several months."

"Okay, okay," I say smiling as I realize just how many clothes I've put on the bed.

"Maybe you can get my uniform and boots from the closet for me," he says.

I go to the closet and get his uniform from a hanger, but as I pick up his boots I knock over a long, thin beige box from its resting place atop a bigger box. Its contents spill onto the floor. I put his uniform aside, his boots on the floor and pick up the spillage. It's the Polaroids that Jim had taken of the three of us having sex when we were first getting together. I had forgotten all about them.

"Jim, I don't know if it's a good idea having these anywhere around," I say, "especially now."

"Well let's take them back to the apartment," he suggests.

"That would make me feel better," I respond.

He puts the contents back in the box and goes to his desk where he tapes it up.

"Hang on to this," he says while he hands it to me. Then he picks up his boots and uniform and takes them over to the bed so everything to go to the apartment can be together. Before I know it Jim has packed a few things into the weekend bag, and is putting his coat on to leave.

"That's it?" I ask.

"If I need anything else I'll come back for it," he says as he zips up his coat.

"Okay," I say as I pick up my coat and put it on.

We leave Jim's room, him with his weekend bag slung over his shoulders and his combat boots in hand, and me with his uniform draped over my arm and the boxful of Polaroids in my hand. We get outside of the building and walk toward my car when Jim says, "wait a minute."

I stop and turn to him.

"I forgot something back in my room. Do you mind taking these to the car?" he asks handing me his weekend bag and boots.

"I'll just be a sec."

He turns and walks quickly back into the building. I go to the car and put everything neatly in the back seat. I get in, start the engine and wait for him to come back. I turn on the radio and listen while the car warms up.

A car pulls up to the barrack and parks in front of the building entrance. A solitary figure gets out. It's Captain Ty Braid, I didn't recognize him at first because he's out of uniform. He's a commanding officer in Jim's squadron, and he's quite an imposing figure. He's tall and muscular with clear bright eyes, and an irresistibly charming smile.

Right now he looks like a man with a mission as he closes and locks his car door and strides toward the barrack. Jim is coming out of the building as Captain Braid approaches it. They nod to each other and Braid says something to Jim. Jim stops and looks back at him as Braid grabs the front door and starts to open it. He lets it go and the two of them smile, move closer together and have a brief conversation.

Braid seems to be doing most of the talking while Jim looks spellbound as he listens and laughs. I watch as Braid places his hand gently on Jim's shoulder. They laugh together, and then Braid heads into the building. Jim comes toward the car, his writing book in-hand.

"You and Braid seem to be on friendly terms," I say to Jim as he gets into the car.

"Yeah, Ty's great," smiles Jim as he closes the door, "I like him."

"Oh, you guys are on a first name basis too?"

"He asked me to call him by his first name when we're out of uniform."

"So this isn't the first time you guys have had conversations?"

"Oh no, we've talked a lot," Jim smiles. Then he pauses and says, "Can I tell you something in confidence?"

"Sure."

"Did you know he's bi?"

"Who told you that?"

"He did."

"When?"

"The night that I saw him at the steam bath.

"When did you see him there?"

"A couple of weeks ago."

"A couple of weeks ago? And you didn't tell Marcel and I you were there?"

Jim sits in stunned silence.

"I," he says pausing for a second, "I didn't see there would be any harm done. I hadn't been in a while and just wanted to see what was happening down there. You're not upset are you?"

"Well, why would you even want to go there?"

There's another pregnant pause, then Jim says, "I'm sorry Bryn. I didn't think."

"That's right, you didn't."

We're silent.

Then Jim says, "I guess my understanding was that even though we're together we have certain freedoms."

"It was my understanding that we're together, period."

We're silent again.

"I'm really sorry, Bryn. I don't know what else to say. I didn't think you would be upset about this."

"Then why didn't you say something to Marcel and I?"

"Because I didn't think it was any big deal."

"Hmmph."

"You okay, Bryn?"

"No."

"C'mon Bryn. We never said that we could never have any extra curricular dalliances."

"Hmmph," I grunt again. "You saw Braid down there, huh?"

"Yeah."

"You guys didn't, you know, do anything that night?"

"No we didn't do anything that night except sit in the TV lounge for a couple of hours and talk."

"Have you guys ever, you know?"

"No, but that's not from Ty's lack of trying."

"He's been trying to get you into bed?"

"Yeah. He's made all kinds of overtures. I've avoided giving him an answer."

"How have you avoided it?"

"Any time he starts on the subject I laugh and pretend he's not serious about it."

I pause again, and then get up enough nerve to ask, "Do you find him attractive?"

Jim is silent for a moment, "Truthfully?"

"Nothing else but."

"Yeah, I guess I do."

A small stinging rush makes me shudder. My heart tells me I don't want to hear any more, but my curiosity gets the better of me.

"Would you go to bed with him?"

"Do you really want to know, Bryn?"

The thought of Jim and Braid in bed together is too much for me. I quickly move on and ask, "So what did you guys talk about that night?"

"Well you know what it's like being gay in the forces. It was like finding a brother in your ranks, especially when he's a commanding officer. We talked about the forces, liking guys, and he joked about the movie that was on the TV at the time." Jim chuckles, "He's got a really neat sense of humour."

"Yeah he probably shakes his weenie at his wife every morning and goes, 'WOO-WOO' on his way to the shower."

"He probably does," Jim says, "It's funny though..."

"What's that?"

"Ty didn't seem interested in anything that was going on at the steam bath that night."

"How do you mean?"

Jim hesitates like he's trying to find the right words. "I noticed that Ty didn't notice any of the other guys who were there that night. He might as well have been sitting at home in his living room alone."

"Maybe he's just used to being there."

"Maybe."

I've had enough and don't want to talk about this anymore. "Well, shall we go then?" I ask.

"Yeah, let's."

I turn the music up a bit as I drive the car onto the road. Both of us are silent as the song on the radio plays, *"New York, London, Paris, Munich, Everybody talk about Pop Music. Talk about, pop music. Talk about, pop music."*

We drive through the main gate of the base and turn onto Crowchild Trail. I feel this sudden sense of loss inside of me, and the only thought in my head is, *Ty Braid, hmmph!*

∞

Braid serves the ball to the back of the opposing team's court. Tony rushes from the back row to set the ball up, Kelly and Bert both go to volley the ball forward and miss. Marcel slides under the ball to keep it in the air, and manages to do so. That's when Chuck barely volleys it over the net, but Lloyd from our team leaps to the top of the net to spike the ball back onto their side. Bert from their team is just as quick, however and returns the spike. The ball hits our court with a tremendous thud! A cheer goes up from their side. Game point.

Three guys on the sidelines are wearing blonde wigs and shaking pompoms in the air, "We're the team that's really tight, and we're so tight we're out of sight! Chick-A-Boom-Chick-A-Boom-Chick-A- Boom!"

"Do they stay up all night making these things up?" I ask Sparky indicating the cheerleaders.

Sparky laughs, "No they make it up as they go along. At least we used to when I was one of the girls."

Meanwhile Jim steps up to take his turn serving the ball, and as he does a chorus of wolf whistles go up from various members of the crowd.

"Marry me Jim!" yells one of the guys from my team.

"Jim, I wanna bear your children!" yells someone else.

"Never mind serving the ball, Jim," yells Braid, "just take off your clothes for us!" Everyone laughs and cheers.

This happens every time Jim goes up to serve the ball. He's one of the most popular guys at these Wednesday night gay volleyball games.

He serves the ball over to our court, and I get underneath it to set it up, that's when Sparky accidentally bumps into me as he's going for the ball as well. The ball hits me on the head, Lloyd tries to retrieve it but it falls to the floor. Game over. Another cheer goes up from their side of the court. Their team has won for the second week in row.

"We'll get you bastards next week!" yells Braid to the opposing team.

"That's what you said last week," Marcel yells back.

The three cheerleaders stand to attention, clasp their hands in front of their chests and break into their weekly rendition of the closing theme to the Carol Burnett Show, *"I'm so glad we had this time together. Just to have a laugh or sing a song..."*

They finish the final two lines of the verse; tug their ear lobes then the two teams disperse while applauding.

"Why did you decide not to be with the cheerleaders anymore?" I ask Sparky.

He hesitates then smiles, "Because I wanted to be butch my dear."

"That explains the blue lace curtains on the back windows of your jeep," Lloyd says while he walks by.

I laugh.

"It's...a fashion statement," smiles Sparky, "It's a fashion statement."

"A fashion statement," Lloyd says glancing back and smiling, "How butch of you."

Sparky laughs.

I look over to the opposing team's court and see that Braid has wasted no time in rushing over to chat Jim up again. This is his third week coming with us to these games, and I for one hate it. So far the impression among the volleyball regulars seems to be mixed about Braid. Some think he's charming and want to seduce him, while others like me think he's an asshole. The few conversations I have had with him always return to one subject—him. So I've made it a point to say very little when I'm around him.

While I watch the two of them, I remember that week in January that Jim and Marcel stayed over at the apartment with me. After my initial reaction regarding Jim going to the steam bath, we had a really great time. Marcel pointed out to me that we had not set any parameters at the beginning of our relationship, so he could see how things could be confused as they were. We agreed that even though we are together, we would have certain freedoms as long as we are living in our own places.

We also decided that Jim should try living in the barracks another month to see if Harrington and Sloan would settle down. If they didn't he would move into the apartment with me. At least then he would only be dealing with them at work. I was secretly hoping Jim would eventually move into the apartment. It appears that both conclusions we reached during that week were mistakes, because when Jim did return to the barrack, Braid began to drop in on him. Every once in a while at first, but then they started meeting off the base more frequently. Now it seems neither Marcel nor I can get near Jim because Braid takes so much of his time.

In retrospect I should have known that would happen, given Jim's response to Braid's appearance that day I helped him get his stuff from the barrack. You know, two months ago I thought the three of us were inseparable, now I'm beginning to wonder if he even thinks about Marcel and me.

"Are you guys coming for a bite?" Sparky asks interrupting my train of thought.

"Oh," I say awaking from my thoughts, "I'll ask the others if they're into it."

"I'm into going for something to eat," Marcel says causing me to jump. "Sorry, I thought you knew that I was behind you. I didn't have any dinner before coming here tonight."

I can see Braid and Jim walking toward us, Braid with his arm around Jim's shoulders.

"A bunch of us are heading out for a bite," I say to them, "You guys gonna come along, or do you want me to give you a lift back to Base?"

"Sure we'll come along, won't we, handsome?" Braid smiles as he gives Jim a squeeze closer to him.

"Sure," Jim smiles.

"Well, let's get our gear and we can get going," says Braid.

Marcel has brought my coat over to me while Jim and Braid go to get their stuff that is unceremoniously heaped in a small bundle in one corner of the gym.

"What does Jim see in that asshole?" I ask Marcel.

"Well, Ty does have his charm,' Marcel sighs.

"What does he give Jim that we don't?"

"You know, Jim," says Marcel, "he's like a wide-eyed puppy. He'll follow anybody around who pays a lot of attention to him and gives him lots of compliments."

"And we don't do that?" I snap as we put on our coats.

"Yeah but look at Ty. He's handsome, he's a commanding officer. You told me once that a lot of people on the Base respect him; and he's attracted to Jim."

"So what? Look, didn't the three of us discuss all of this? I thought we had something meaningful. Doesn't he care about us anymore? Can't he see this gets to us?"

"Bryn, you're right. We did discuss this, but what more can we really do about it? Jim is a man of many whims, you know that. He always goes off on these flights of fancy. He insists they're just buddies and haven't done anything."

"Not yet," I say, "I mean look at them Marcel, it's just a matter of time."

"We did agree that we have certain freedoms as long as we live apart"

"But this is carrying it too far," I say as we reach the gym door. "Are they together or what? Isn't Braid married with a couple of kids? Does he really believe his wife doesn't suspect something is up with all the time they spend together?"

"Bryn you're starting to get loud, calm down. We don't know any of that."

I realize that I am beginning to raise my voice a bit, and in total embarrassment I shut up.

Braid and Jim have retrieved their gear and join us as we're walking out of the building to the parking lot.

"Hey Bryn," Jim says, "Have you heard that Harrington and Sloan have both suddenly been posted to other Bases?"

"I did hear something about that," I quietly say.

"Yeah," Jim continues, "They're gone. It happened so fast even they weren't expecting it.

"Isn't that a coincidence," says Marcel, "the two guys who were giving you trouble have suddenly been posted away."

"It's not a coincidence," says Braid.

"What do you mean?" asks Marcel.

"That's why I like being in charge. If I see something going on that I don't like, I have the power to change it."

The sound of our shoes as we trudge through the hardened snow is the only thing that is heard for a moment. Then Marcel says, "I'm not sure what you mean Ty?"

"I saw what Harrington and Sloan were up to giving handsome here a hard time and didn't like it. So I made arrangements for those two to take a fast trip away from Calgary for a couple of years."

"Really?" Jim exclaims his face beaming, "you got rid of them because of what they were doing to me?"

We reach my car while Braid answers, "That's right, handsome. Sloan's in Petawawa and Harrington's in Edmonton because I didn't like what they were doing to you. So you owe me," he smiles and winks.

We get into the car, Marcel in the passenger seat, and Jim and Braid in the back. Marcel asks, "So has there been any more trouble around you being gay, Jim?"

"No, it's been quiet."

"And if there is any trouble," says Braid, "I'll find out who it is and they'll be gone too." Then he snaps his fingers and says, "To the restaurant driver and make it snappy."

I turn and give him a mock salute.

"And just you remember that, Lieutenant," Braid sanctimoniously quips.

Marcel gives me a look that says, *This guy's a dickhead.* I start the car and we leave the parking lot heading downtown.

∞

The Combo House is one of the few restaurants in this town that's open 24 hours. It's within walking distance of the Parkside, so a lot of the patrons that visit during the evening and early morning hours are gay, especially during the weekends.

The wait staff put together several tables for the bunch of us. Surrounded by a swirl of conversation and laughter, the four of us are seated opposite each other near one end of the row. Our empty plates lay in front of us waiting to be collected. I look across the table at Jim and Braid. Jim has been totally engrossed in anything that Braid has to say tonight, no matter how pontificating or imbecilic it is.

"Are you guys going to the GIRC Dance this Saturday night?" Lloyd asks us.

Braid laughs, "The what?"

"The GIRC Dance," Marcel repeats while putting out his after-meal cigarette.

"And just what the hell is a GIRC? Besides the noise an ostrich might make," Braid continues as he becomes really obnoxious by loudly making an annoying, "GIIIRC… GIIIRC… GIIIRC."

The only one laughing is Jim.

"GIRC," explains Lloyd, "stands for Gay Information Resources Calgary. They hold a dance every month."

"Yeah," continues Marcel, "They're lots of fun and really well attended."

"And just where are these alleged dances held," Braid smirks.

"The Alexandra Centre," Marcel answers.

"The Alexandra Centre," Braid repeats, "Never heard of it. Where is it?"

"It's on 9th Avenue South East over in Inglewood," says Lloyd.

"And the best thing of all," says Jim, "it's always word of mouth that gets people out. So people who don't usually go to the gay clubs, go to these dances every month."

"Really?" Braid asks.

"Really," Jim affirms.

"Like who?"

"Like for instance oil company execs and military personnel."

He has a look of serious consideration in his eyes. Then he asks Jim, "Are you going to this dance?"

"Yeah," Jim replies, "I always go with these guys."

That serious look turns to a spark in Braid's eyes and an evil smile slowly cuts across his mouth. Seeing the look on Braid's face reminds me of Boris Karloff reciting, *The Grinch had a wonderfully awful idea.*

"The wife and I are supposed to be taking our monthly trip to Red Deer this weekend to see her folks," Braid says, casting his evil grin at Jim. "It looks like she'll have to drive up alone with the kids this time because I'm suddenly busy and can't go."

Then Marcel waves his arm in the air toward the restaurant entrance. Howard smiles as he stands at the entrance then sachets over to us.

"You've dyed your hair," Marcel says.

"You like it, dear?" Howard smiles while primping the back of his hair, "I decided the Marilyn Monroe bottled blonde look is passé."

"It makes you look younger for some reason," says Marcel.

"You're going home alone, Bryn," Howard says to me with a smile, "Marcel's mine tonight."

Braid is quietly staring at Howard.

"Howard," says Marcel, "this is Ty. Ty this is Howard."

"Oh another handsome soldier?" Howard squeals as he stretches his hand to Braid.

"That's right ma'am," Braid smiles.

"My goodness is it just me," Howard says with a southern accent while fanning himself with his hand, "Or do they got those li'l ol' ovens in the kitchen turned way up tonight?"

"That's just how a real man affects women," Braid says.

I think, "*What an asshole.*"

Howard stops and looks at Braid for a moment. "Anyway," he says turning his attention back to Marcel, "I thought I'd pop in to see who was here before I head home."

A couple of the waiters are handing out bills for the food, and some of the guys at the table are putting their jackets on.

"You got here just as everyone is leaving," says Jim.

"Yeah," I agree, "It's almost 11 and 6:30 always comes too early in the morning for me."

"Well," Howard sighs, "I guess it's Cinderella time pour moi aussi. Are you guys going to the dance as usual this weekend?"

"Oh we'll be there," Marcel smiles.

"I guess I'll have to decide what to wear," Howard says as he flits his hands.

"Why don't you wear your sequined evening gown, sweetheart?" Braid sarcastically quips with a smirk on his face.

"It's at the cleaners dear," Howard plays along. "Besides, that was last month's dance."

"We'll see you Saturday night then Howard," Marcel smiles as he zips up his ski jacket.

"Oh definitely."

"And sweetheart," says Braid, "I hope you'll use the ladies entrance when you arrive."

"Only if accompanied by a real man such as y'all," Howard replies in his mock-Scarlett O'Hara voice. "In fact honey," Howard continues batting his eyelashes, "You're such a real man, why don't y'all come over to my place before the dance. I've got a beautiful whorehouse red mini-skirt that would fit you perfectly. That is if you still plan on accompanying me through the ladies entrance."

That smirk is instantly erased from Braid's face as everyone within earshot chuckles.

"Let's go," a suddenly disgusted Braid grumbles to me as he grabs his jacket and heads for the door.

"Thank you for that," I whisper to Howard, "He's been getting on my nerves all night."

Howard smiles and blows me a kiss. We say our goodnights and leave.

∞

At Braid's insistence we drop him and Jim off at a city transit stop on an overpass opposite the main entrance of the Base. As we drive back on to Crowchild Trail, I look in the rear view mirror and watch the two of them. They're standing talking with each other as they fade from my view.

"I think Jim had better be careful around Ty," Marcel says. "I don't know what it is, but after tonight there's something about that guy I don't like."

"Aside from the fact he's an asshole?"

"Yeah."

"Maybe we should have a talk with Jim this weekend."

"Yeah," says Marcel, "If we can keep Ty away from him long enough."

∞

As usual the Alexandra Centre is filled with people, chatter, laughter, and music. Folding tables and chairs are stretched across almost the entire width of this room filling two-thirds of the floor space. The final third of this former school gym is open for dancing. Ken the disc jockey is centre on the stage in the front of the gym while two drag queens dance on either side of him. They are dressed like go-go dancers with beehive hairdos of exaggerated height, white go-go boots and matching black and white, one-piece mini skirts. Strangely enough, their manner of dress seems to fit right in with this new wave craze that's going on right now. This is like a really bad wedding.

Ken's music crosses from disco, to new wave, to country, to rock and back again. An almost entirely new stream of people goes up to dance as the various types of music are played. The women seem to prefer country music and anything by Anne Murray, the older guys seem to prefer the rock'n'roll from the fifties and early sixties, and the drag queens seem to cling to the disco.

I don't dance very much, but Marcel has me up dancing to a song called *Jet Boy, Jet Girl*. As the end of the song approaches and it starts to fade, the opening chords of *Making Plans for Nigel* by XTC begins. I know it's that song because Marcel has been playing it a lot at the apartment lately. A chorus of screams goes up from a group of young people in the crowd, and brightly clothed new wave types rapidly surround us.

Two young guys take their place immediately to our right and begin to jump up and down in one spot, *pogoing*, I think they call it.

Their mode of dress is typical of the way that most of the New Wavers I see adorn themselves. One of them is wearing tight black straight-legged jeans, and the other is wearing a bright orange baggy pair of pants with small cuffs on the legs. Both have plimsoles on their feet. They sport brightly-coloured, long-sleeved shirts with narrow collars and dark narrow ties around their necks. Their hair is cut short and spikey, and one has green tips at the end of his spikes.

Marcel is really getting into the music, pogoing just like the guys beside me. I'm feeling out-of-place and slightly embarrassed because I don't know if I should be doing the same as everyone else or not.

I put my hand on Marcel's shoulder, "Look, I think I'll sit this one out," I say loudly in his ear to be heard above the music.

"Sure, old man," he smiles at me.

We shuffle off the dance floor dodging New Wavers as we go.

"Do you want another drink?" he asks.

"Sure," I say searching my pockets for a liquor ticket.

"That's okay, I'll get this round," he says as he heads to the line-up.

I head over to the spot where Jim and Braid sit. I stop to watch them momentarily. Jim is looking especially handsome tonight with his green Lacoste Alligator shirt and his 501 jeans that beautifully accentuate his ass. Braid on the other hand sits back in his chair like some kind of lord with his arm around Jim.

He quietly surveys the entire scene. He'll watch everything for a couple of minutes and then say something to Jim. Jim laughs, Braid smirks, Braid watches the scene, says something to Jim, Jim laughs, Braid smirks. He really fucking annoys me. That fucker's bad news, I just know it. So I clear my throat, take a deep breath and approach them.

"Are you guys having a good time?" I politely smile.

"As long as I've got handsome here by my side, I'm happy," Braid says. Then he tickles Jim. Jim laughs and resists Braid's tickling like an innocent boy.

This is too much for me. I look over to the liquor line-up and see Marcel talking with Howard, Mark, and Honker. Marcel notices me looking their way and motions me to join them.

"I'm going to go and chat with Marcel and the other guys," I say to Jim and Braid.

"Take your time, Lieutenant," says Braid while looking at Jim. I smile politely and walk away from them while mumbling, "*bastard*," under my breath. I join the others.

"Are you okay?" Marcel asks.

I look back at Braid and Jim. I grit my teeth and growl, "What a pompous—"

"Hey, be careful," says Marcel, "Don't let your eyes burn holes in Ty because they just might burn Jim as well."

"There aren't enough cuss words in the world to do that fucker justice," I say with disgust.

"Here's your drink," Marcel says. "I've never seen you this upset before."

The song ends, the music stops, and people go back to their seats. A spotlight shines onto the emptying dance floor, and a man enters the spot carrying a microphone. He's tall and thin with a receding hairline and a neatly cropped beard. He's dressed in a black leather jacket, black pants and shoes, a white shirt with a thin black tie.

"Good evening ladies and gentlemen," he says, "Welcome to the March 1980 edition of the Gay Information and Resources Calgary Community Dance."

A round of applause goes up from the audience.

"My name is Dennis, and I'll be your emcee for the next hour. So order up another drink, sit back, and enjoy the show. Let's get right to the first act of the evening. Please put your hands together for everyone's favourite little girl, WANDA JUNE!"

The spotlight is instantly whisked from Dennis to stage right where a tall overweight drag queen dressed as Shirley Temple skips to the centre of the dance floor to the opening chords of *My Boy Lollipop*. She turns her back to the audience, lifts her dress and shakes her corpulent, underwear-clad butt at us.

"Oh Mary!" Honker screams, "Acres of cellulite!"

"Why do the gay guys in this town call each other Mary?" I ask Mark.

"I don't know, Matilda," Mark replies, "Why *do* the gay guys in this town call each other Mary?" I roll my eyes. Mark gives me a grin. I go back to watching Wanda June. But I'm distracted by the sound of Braid's laughter; which I can hear above all else. I look his direction. He's laughing loudly and pointing toward the stage. His other arm still wrapped tightly around Jim. I look back to the dance floor where Wanda June is skipping around the perimeter squeezing the women's tits and grabbing the guys' crotches.

Honker is cheering Wanda on, "That's right Wanda! Go for it! WOOOOO!!"

Braid's laughter echoes in my ears as if Satan himself is laughing at me. The end of the song quickly fades as Wanda June skips back off the dance floor stage right to applause.

The spotlight moves back to Dennis who says, "C'mon, let's hear it for Wanda June!" The audience roars applause while Wanda takes a final bow just to the right of the stage.

"Okay, before we get into the show I've got a couple of announcements here," says Dennis. "There are still lots of volunteer opportunities for the National Gay and Lesbian Conference at the University of Calgary this summer. We need help in all areas especially billeting of conference attendants. So if you have a spare room, bed or sofa, we would appreciate hearing from you. You can call us at the G.I.R.C. office—"

"GIIIIIRRRRRC!" yells Braid, followed by a trickle of laughter in the crowd. I bury my face in my hand, I feel embarrassed for the asshole. But Dennis moves on.

"There will be another training session for those who are interested in being volunteers for the Gay Phone Line. You can call Richard at the G.I.R.C. office if you want more information. By the way, there are leaflets up here on the stage for you to take if you want to volunteer for the conference or for the phone line sessions. They have all of the phone numbers and info on them."

I feel Marcel's arms around me. I turn my head to look at him. He smiles at me, "Bryn, you seem to be forgetting something."

"What's that?"

"I'm still here," he smiles.

That statement hits me like a cast iron skillet. I smile in return and hold him close to me.

"Okay, enough business," says Dennis, "Now back to the entertainment.

"She's back here in Calgary in spite of public opinion. Please welcome all the way from her island in Hawaii, PRAIRIE PRINCESS WANNA-LAYA!"

I break our embrace in surprise. Why does that name sound familiar?

The spotlight swings over to stage left where a tall thin drag queen moves to centre stage. Oh my God! That's why the name sounds familiar. It's Howard, and he's dressed in the same outfit that he wore to Mark and Honker's Stampede party in the summer.

He has his red sequined western hat that is still dangling precariously from atop his white beehive hairdo, with a pair of rhinestone, cats-eye sunglasses peering from underneath. He sports the same white blouse with a multi-coloured plastic Hawaiian Lei around his neck, and a red sequined vest with a long grass skirt. He shakes his hips like he's doing the Hula, and he strums a ukelele to the opening chords of, *"If you like Ukelele lady, ukelele lady like you..."*

Marcel looks at me, rolls his eyes and grins, "We still rue the day he went to Honolulu."

For the first time tonight, I feel an amused smile on my face. I look to the place where Howard stood only a couple of minutes before, then I look at Marcel in disbelief.

"How did Howard get changed so fast?"

"He was wearing the same things he's wearing now."

"Look, I would have noticed if he was wearing that."

"It was covered by the big black coat he was wearing."

"Was he wearing a big black coat?"

"Yes, and if you hadn't been so busy being pissed off at Ty, you would have seen Howard go up to the side of the dance floor, take of his coat and put his wig and hat on."

"Oh."

I look back to the stage and quietly watch Howard perform. The audience is clapping and cheering Howard on. Marcel nudges my elbow. I glance at him and he motions toward Braid and Jim. They're kissing, very passionately. Braid holds the back of Jim's head as they press their faces together. I'm reminded of a wolf devouring a lamb.

Then I feel Marcel's embrace once more. "Ya Know what?" he asks.

"What."

"I love you, Mr. Menzies," he says as he caresses my cheek.

I smile and embrace him. "I love you too, Mr. Arsenault." We kiss, and this feels really good to be in Marcel's arms.

Then I feel a tap on my shoulder. I turn around to see Jim smiling at me.

"We're leaving now," he says with a wild sparkle in his eyes.

"Oh, you're not coming back with us?" I say to deliberately get a reaction from him.

Jim looks surprised at my remark.

"Aren't you with us?" I demand.

Now Jim looks like I've slapped him in the face.

"Jim have a good time tonight," Marcel interrupts as he kisses Jim. Then he turns to me and whispers, "C'mon Bryn, quit acting like a jealous queen. What can we really do about this?"

I snort in disgust because I realize that Marcel's right again. I look at Jim and say, "I'm sorry Jim, and have a good time tonight." I try to convince myself that I really mean it.

Jim and I kiss, then I whisper in his ear, "Look, be careful."

"What do you mean?"

"Just… do that."

"Do what?" Braid asks as he joins us carrying their coats.

"Just have a good time." I say through my teeth.

"Don't worry, Lieutenant. I'm taking this young officer back to my quarters so he can submit to some discipline." Then he grabs Jim and turns him around. "Look at that ass!" he says giving Jim a little slap, "You're gonna get it tonight."

Jim's face brightens again.

"It was a good suggestion coming here this evening, Lieutenant. I'll probably be back next month."

Inwardly I cringe at the thought. They put on their coats and bid their good nights.

"C'mon handsome I can't wait to get you home," Braid smiles. The two of them turn without another word and quickly head out the door. I stare at the door after their exit.

I don't know what I'm feeling now, anger or fear.

"Do you want to go back to the apartment?" Marcel asks.

I look at him and nod my head. "You drive," is all I can say.

∞

Watching events unfold this month have me glued to the television and buying newspapers every day. I'll always remember May 1980 as being a month of dramatic events in North America.

Rene Levesque and this referendum on Quebec separation has been scary to watch. Knowing a lot of French speaking people, I can understand them not feeling like they're understood by the rest of Canada; and being in love with Marcel, who is staunchly, "Je suis Acadie," (I am Acadian), I've been watching his reactions particularly.

"I can understand The Quebecois wanting to separate," he said to me while we were watching TV the night of the referendum.

"Well...I guess you would because you're so proudly Acadian."

"We share a lot with the Quebecois, but our culture remains strong because we like to share it with others."

"René Lévesque says that the Quebecois are surrounded by the English culture in North America and need to protect themselves," I point out. "He says that the French culture is in danger of becoming history."

"Maybe he says that to illustrate how they feel," Marcel responded, "It's up to them to try to make the rest of North America understand where they're coming from. If they don't, they might end up being just a historical society. We Acadians have a strong bond with the Cajuns, not only because we're of the same blood, but because we all invite others in to enjoy our culture with us. That way others see the value in keeping the culture alive. Just like the Québecois are trying to do with English Canada."

"But English Canada understands," I said.

"Oh yeah?" Marcel responded. "Do I have to remind you of that incident at the liquor store three weeks ago?"

My mind was cast back to that time in the local liquor store, when Marcel wore a t-shirt that simply said Montréal. A short stocky man with a trucker's cap that said *Muffdive* across it, scowled at him and yelled, "Montreal! Where the hell is that?" He seemed to be itching for some kind of spat. Marcel said nothing, but he was upset, and told me so when we got back home.

I said nothing and turned my attention back to the TV just on time to see Monsieur Lévesque standing at the podium smiling at the crowd in Montreal, but with tears streaming down his face. The results of the referendum had come in and the "yes" side had been defeated.

"Having said all of that," Marcel continued, "if anybody should be holding a referendum on separation from Canada, it should be the Natives. The white people have never been very nice to them."

"True enough," I said.

Yes, it's been a busy month for news, but what's been on the television hasn't been the only news of late, Jim has become a part of our lives once more. Little by little, over the past couple of months, he has spent more time with us. In fact, he just left here about an hour ago to go back to the barrack. He was here for the weekend and took the bus back because Marcel and I were too lazy to get out of bed to drive him. Jim says Braid told him that his wife began asking questions about where's he's been and who he's been with, so he's had to spend more time at home. That suits me just fine. The latest news about that creep is that he's been seconded to Base Borden for a month and he left just this week. His parting did seem pretty quick though. Suddenly Braid was gone to Borden, just as

quickly as Harrington and Sloan. I'm glad to be rid of him, even if
it is only for a month.

Meanwhile, this was one of the best weekends the three of us
had spent in a long time. All we did was lay in bed together and
watch TV right from the six o'clock news on Friday night, to Bugs
Bunny and coffee yesterday morning, to the breaking news that's
coming from Washington State.

As of 8:30 this morning Mount Saint Helen has erupted. We've
had the Spokane television station on just to get the immediacy of
what's going on down there. They've been repeating a series of still
photos showing a landslide on its north slope, then the initial explo-
sion. The following photos are gradually filled by nothing but black
smoke. It's the most dramatic footage I've seen since the old film of
the Hindenburg exploding in New Jersey back in the '30s. It's about
noon hour, and they've just finished a piece on an old timer named
Harry Truman.

Old Harry owned Mt. St. Helen's Lodge on the north base of
the mountain and gained some local notoriety in refusing to move
in spite of the dire warnings from the authorities to clear out. They
showed an interview they did with the crusty old bugger just a
couple of weeks ago in which he said that he had a talk with The
Lord, and if that's how he meets his end, that's how he meets his
end. He was killed in the eruption. In spite of all the warnings to
campers over the last couple of weeks, the authorities estimate there
were probably 60 to 80 of them in the immediate area as well. As
yet, none of them have been heard from.

The station has been carrying live footage of what's happening in places like Yakima Washington, where the smoke from the
volcano is so thick that the entire town is enshrouded in black.

"Do you want another coffee?" I ask Marcel.

He holds out his cup to me smiling. I take his cup, go into the
kitchen and empty the remaining contents of the pot into both
cups. That's when the phone rings, and Marcel answers it.

"Hello. Oh hi, Jim… Why are you calling from a phone booth? What? Jim, calm down, what's happened?"

I come back into the bedroom, place our cups on the night table and get back in bed.

"Who broke into your room? What's the S.I.U.?"

My heart stops, my back stiffens, and without thinking I grab the phone from Marcel's hand as panic hits me like a slap in the face.

"Jim, what the fuck is going on?"

"Bryn, I'm in deep shit." There's traffic noise in the background that almost drowns the sound of Jim's voice.

"The S.I.U. got into my room, Bryn," he says sounding like he's both out of breath and sobbing.

"Look, how do you know it was the S.I.U.?"

"You remember Dan Kent, the guy across the hall from me?"

"Yeah."

"He told me that he watched them enter my room yesterday afternoon. But he didn't know how to get hold of me to tell me."

I can feel my heart racing and my hands begin to shake.

"Bryn, we really need to talk," Jim sobs.

"Okay where are you, and we'll come to get you."

"I'm at a phone booth in front of an ice cream store at the corner of, ah, 42nd Avenue and 20th Street South West"

"Okay, we'll be right over to get you," I hang up the phone.

"Bryn you're shaking," Marcel says as he rubs his hand up and down my arm.

He's right because I'm spooked.

"What's the S.I.U.?" he asks.

"The Special Investigations Unit. They're an arm of the Military police, and they get involved in your personal affairs if they think there's been a serious violation of conduct."

"Such as?"

"Such as if they suspect you of taking illegal drugs or if they suspect you're homosexual."

Marcel pauses, "Does that mean Jim could get thrown out of the military?"

"Very possibly."

"Oh shit."

"Oh shit is right."

"We'd better go get him," Marcel says, "before he drives himself crazy waiting for us."

∞

We arrive at the corner to see Jim leaning against the side of a one-storey building that stands beside a small parking lot. A large sign painted on the wall of the building says, *My Favourite Ice Cream Parlour*. He has one hand in his pocket while he smokes what's left of a cigarette in the other.

He sees us, tosses the cigarette butt away and approaches the car. As he gets closer I notice his eyes are red like he's been rubbing them, or crying, or both. I get out of the passenger seat and get into the back. Jim gets in and closes the door. The three of us are silent.

"So you've started smoking again," Marcel gently smiles.

Jim shakes his head, "I'm scared."

I reach from the back seat to rub Jim's shoulders, while Marcel does the same from where he sits.

"Tell us what happened," I say.

"I got back this morning and noticed the door to my room was open a bit. I thought that was weird because I always lock it when I leave. So I walked in and noticed that everything looked the same as when I left it, except the drawer of my night table had been left open. Then that's when Dan appeared from across the hall and told me the S.I.U. were in my room yesterday. I looked in the drawer and discovered that something was missing. I guess I panicked and ran all the way over here to phone you as soon as I realized what had happened."

"Okay, let's step back a bit," I say, "Why would the S.I.U. want to focus on you in the first place?"

Jim is silent.

"Do they know you're gay?" Marcel asks.

Jim nods his head, "I guess they do now." Then he turns to me and says, "Because they knew exactly what to look for and where to go to get it."

There's a stunned silence in the car. I stop rubbing his back.

"Jim, I don't like the sound of that. What was it they were after?" I ask, unsure that I really want to know.

Then Marcel puts the car in gear and says, "Let's go. We can talk back at the apartment."

∞

Jim sits on the couch while Marcel sits beside him with his arm around him. I'm pacing back and forth with my hands clenched behind my back like a lawyer in a courtroom drama.

"Jim, you said that the S.I.U. knew exactly what they wanted and where to get it."

Jim nods his head.

"What were they looking for?"

"An envelope."

"What was in the envelope?"

He pauses for a moment and then says, "Polaroids."

I stop cold. "Please tell me that we are not talking about the same Polaroids that were in that beige box in your closet."

Jim is silent.

"Jim, please tell me that all of those Polaroids are here at the apartment, and there weren't any left at the barracks."

Jim is still silent as he looks at me like a scared puppy.

"So you kept some of those Polaroids," Marcel says.

Jim nods again, "In the drawer of my night table."

I take a really deep breath to try to remain calm. "So are you telling us the S.I.U. now have Polaroids of the three of us having sex?"

"You're not in them Bryn," Jim says quietly. "But some of them were pictures that you took."

"But," Marcel interjects, "how did this S.I.U. know what they were looking for?" Jim pulls his body into himself in a fetal position.

"Furthermore," I continue, "Why the hell did you keep some in your room? Didn't I tell you it wasn't a good idea?"

"More importantly though," Marcel says, "how did this S.I.U. know where to go to get them?"

"Stop it!" Jim raises his voice. "Stop interrogating me!"

Marcel and I look at each other. Marcel shakes his head.

Jim regains his composure, takes a deep breath and says, "Ty knew about those Polaroids."

Marcel rolls his eyes and looks away from Jim.

"What?" I say.

"You showed Ty those Polaroids?" Marcel asks.

Jim nods his head.

"Oh that's just great!" I say, "How many other people did you show them to?"

"Only Ty."

"When did you show him those photos?" asks Marcel.

Jim looks at me, then back to Marcel. "It was the day after that G.I.R.C. dance in March. Ty came back to the barracks from his place and wanted to come into my room to talk, so we did."

"What did you talk about," I ask, "that would make you show him those photos?"

"He started to talk about guys at the baths that he's seen and guys on the base that he thought were sexy. And he told me he thought I was handsome and wanted to know the kind of things I like to do in bed."

"Didn't he already know from the night of the GIRC Dance" Marcel asks.

"No," Jim says sheepishly, "We didn't do anything that night." There's a long pause.

"Just what do you mean, *we didn't do anything*?" I ask.

"We got back to his place that night and he told me that he was feeling guilty because we were going to have sex in the bed that he and his wife share. So I told him we didn't have to use the bedroom, we could have sex anywhere."

Jim pauses.

"And," I continue.

"And then Ty said he was feeling tired anyway. So he told me that because he was feeling guilty, and was tired why didn't we try some other time. He drove me back to the barracks."

"Didn't that strike you kind of funny that he would be hot after your ass all this time, and then when he has his chance, you end up sleeping back at the barrack by yourself?" I ask.

"It did strike me strange at the time, but on the other hand I didn't find the things he was saying unreasonable."

"Getting back to the Polaroids," Marcel says, "he wanted to know what you liked to do in bed, then what?"

"So Jim thought he'd just whip out those photos and show him what we do together," I say beginning to feel angry by the whole thing.

"No, that's not the way it was," says Jim. "He wanted to know if I had any boyfriends, so I told him about us."

"Oh great," I say, "so he does know about the relationship the three of us have."

Jim nods his head.

"Bryn, just let him finish," Marcel says.

"Ty seemed to think that we have a really great arrangement and started asking all kinds of questions about us."

"Like what kind of questions?" Marcel asks.

"Like where I spent my weekends, what we did in bed together, were there any more photos he could look at, and if we knew any other gay soldiers."

"And of course you answered them," I say.

"Yes," Jim says quietly.

"Did you show him any more Polaroids like he wanted you to?" asks Marcel.

"No."

I'm beginning to feel sick. With each question that Jim answers I've got a sinking feeling that gets deeper and deeper.

"Jim," Marcel says softly, "I don't understand how you could be so free with all this information, knowing how it might affect your career, not to mention Bryn's career."

Jim bows his head, "I'm so sorry, Bryn."

"It's too late for apologies, Jim," I say, "that's not helping. We've got to figure out what to do now."

"I thought he was for real guys," Jim continues, "he was at the baths, he came with us to the volleyball games and a couple of the G.I.R.C. dances, he and I talked for hours about being gay, or bi or whatever. We kissed a lot, I thought I could trust him."

"And now," Marcel says, "this S.I.U. has got Polaroid's of you, and suddenly Ty's been stationed out of the province for a month, just long enough for the authorities to swoop in to get you. Don't you see what's happened Jim? Ty was a plant."

Jim bows his head again and says, "I thought he was one of us."

Marcel looks at Jim and says, "It looks like this S.I.U. does their homework really well."

I sit beside Jim. "We told you to be careful, Jim," I say. "We said there was something about him that wasn't quite right."

"What's going to happen now?" Marcel asks.

I breathe a deep sigh. "I hate to think, Marcel," I say, "I hate to think."

∞

I glance at the young corporal sitting at the desk watching me. He has a bit of a smirk on his face as if to say, *I know what this is about and I know what you've been up to.* He points at my commanding officer's office door.

"He's expecting you," he says.

I knock on the door.

"Come in," says my Commanding Officer.

I open the door, "You wanted to see me, sir?"

"Yes, Lieutenant Menzies," he says while he stands by a window with his back to me, "Come in and shut the door."

I do so. He turns to me and points to a chair in front of his desk. "Please sit down."

I do.

"Lieutenant Menzies, I've received some disturbing news from the S.I.U. about somebody that you are known to associate with on a regular basis. You do know Lieutenant James Whitelaw, don't you?

"Yes, sir."

"Would you say he's a close personal friend of yours?"

"Yes, sir."

"Are you aware that the S.I.U. entered his quarters on the weekend and now have photos in their possession showing Lieutenant Whitelaw engaged in homosexual acts?"

I swallow hard. "Yes, sir, I am aware of this."

"Were you also aware that the S.I.U. had employed a well respected officer to gauge Lieutenant Whitelaw's activities for the last three months?"

"No, sir," I lie, and my C.O. moves over in front of where I'm sitting and leans on his desk.

"Lieutenant Menzies, you're name is mentioned all the way through this officer's report. He claims to have seen you at places where homosexuals gather and reports that you have many friends who are homosexual."

I'm dying inside.

"He also reports that, according to Lieutenant Whitelaw, you, he and a civilian are involved in a three-way homosexual relationship. Is any of this true, Lieutenant?"

I want to say no. I want to deny any knowledge of Jim. I want to run out of the building and drive as far my car will take me, but I quietly say, "Yes, sir."

"All of this is true then?"

"Yes, sir."

He looks at the floor and strokes his grey beard then says, "Do you understand that Lieutenant Whitelaw will have to go before a tribunal?"

"Yes, sir."

"Do you also understand that since your name is included throughout the S.I.U. report that you will have to go before that same tribunal?"

"I do now, sir."

"Do you further understand that I will have to inform the tribunal of your answers to me just now?"

I swallow hard again, "Yes, sir."

He looks off into space for a moment as if thinking about what has just been said. He looks at me and says, "Bryn, I like you. You're a hell of a junior officer, and you have a good long career ahead of you. Now I don't give a shit what you do in your personal life. But I hate like hell to see this type of indiscretion stand in your way. Now I can't promise you anything, but I'll see what I can do for you. I'll be putting in a good word to the tribunal for you as your Commanding Officer, and the rest is up to them."

"Thank you, sir, I appreciate that."

He gets up and pats my shoulder then he takes his place behind his desk, "That's all I have to say, Lieutenant. Any questions?"

"Well, how did the S.I.U. suspect Lieutenant Whitelaw of being homosexual in the first place, sir?"

My C.O. raises his eyebrows and then says, "Apparently they received a heads up from a couple of other junior officers who were in the same barrack block as Lieutenant Whitelaw."

"May I ask their identities, sir?"

"I can't tell you that, Lieutenant. But what I will say is that you knew them and they were both posted to other bases back in January."

Just as I thought, Harrington and Sloan were directly involved.

"What's going to happen to Lieutenant Whitelaw, sir?"

He leans back in his chair and fiddles with his pen while considering my question, "His prospects don't look very good, I'm afraid. The tribunal will consider those photos of him damaging evidence. I have no idea what kind of penalty they'll impose, but what I can tell you is they will consider this a serious breach of behaviour. And that's all I know. Is that all?"

"Yes, sir."

"I'll be letting you know where the tribunal is and when you are to appear."

The two of us are momentarily silent. "If there is nothing further you may go, Lieutenant."

"Yes, sir."

I stand, salute him and turn to leave.

"And Lieutenant Menzies."

"Yes, sir?"

He folds his hands on top of his desk, "I want to tell you how sorry I am that your name is being dragged through this mess. I don't think you deserve it."

"Thank you, sir."

∞

The clacking of a typewriter from another room is all I can hear as I sit awaiting the tribunal. Ten long minutes have gone by, and though I can hear signs of life all around me, I am the only person present in the hallway. A pair of double doors to my right is where the tribunal is gathering as I wait. My heartbeat seems to echo down this empty hall, and I can't stop my right hand from shaking a little.

How did it ever come to this? Why do I feel like I'm on trial for somebody else?

I was briefed yesterday on who would be on this tribunal: Major Winfield who is Jim's Commanding Officer will be presiding, my Commanding Officer Captain Butler will be there, along with Medical Officer Warren and Captain Whelan of the S.I.U. I was also briefed that Jim and I would be marched into the proceedings just like prisoners.

Over the last two days I've become very resentful of what's taken place. I've especially grown resentful of Jim. Damn him! How could he not have known that having those pictures in his possession might eventually get him and me a lot of unwanted attention? Or did he just not care?

The florescent light from the ceiling momentarily catches my cap badge as my hat lays on my lap drawing my attention to it. It seems to flash me a smile saying, You'll be okay. I can only hope it's right because I feel like I'm about to climb the thirteen steps to the gallows.

I'm startled as the door to the building opens and slams shut. Against the sunlit glass of the doors, a lone silhouette comes up the hall toward me, it's Jim, the last person I want to see right now. He walks over and for a moment stands in front of me. I look up at him. His eyes are full of scared puppy emotion then he sits beside me.

"Bryn," he says in a low voice.

"Don't talk to me," I say in a stern but equally low voice.

"Bryn, please."

"I said don't talk to me."

Jim bows his head then continues, "I'm so sorry about this, Bryn. I wish—"

"Stop right there, Jim. Are you really sorry about all of this? How could you have not have known those photos might eventually lead to trouble? Especially when you showed them to Braid?"

"I know Bryn and—"

"No, no, you don't know. You don't know how humiliated I feel right now."

"Isn't there anything I can do?"

"Jim, nothing you could ever say or do could rectify this." I pause then add, "I don't want to see you anymore Jim."

Jim is horrorstruck, "Bryn, please—"

"Look, wasn't it you who decided that Braid was the flavour of the month and went chasing him? Did you stop to think how Marcel and I felt then? And did you really believe that if the shit hit the fan I wouldn't be drawn into it somehow? I asked you not to show any photos to anybody, and the next thing I know Braid knows everything there is to know about us. You didn't stop to think about Marcel and me then, did you? I don't want to see you anymore."

Just then the double doors beside us swing open. My heart stops. We look up to see two Military Policemen, the metallic sound of cleats on the soles of their boots hitting the floor with precision sounds like a death sentence looming. They stand at attention on either side of the doorway.

"Lieutenant James Whitelaw, Lieutenant Bryn Menzies, fall in," commands the one of them. Jim and I reluctantly rise and take our places between them. The command to march is given by the first policeman, and the four of us march into the room where the tribunal sits stern-faced.

We're marched to a small table facing a larger one where the tribunal sits.

"At ease," says Major Winfield.

Jim and I stand at ease while the two guards take a couple of steps back.

"Take you seats," Major Winfield orders.

We sit.

"Lieutenant James Michael Whitelaw," begins the Major, "Pursuant to Section 163 of the National Defence Act, your actions have precipitated this service tribunal. You are being charged under Article 103.25 (c), Scandalous Conduct by an Officer. Charges of your homosexuality were brought before me when I received complaints from Lieutenants Robert Harrington and Michael Sloan. They claimed that on several occasions you had made sexual advances to them—"

"I deny those claims, sir," Jim protests.

Major Winfield removes his glasses, "You will get your chance to speak, Lieutenant."

"My apologies, sir."

The Major puts his glasses on once more and continues. "Acting on these claims I contacted Captain Whelan of the Special Investigations Unit to become involved. Captain Whelan would you like to say a few words?"

Captain Whelan, a large blond man, looks over to Major Winfield and says, "I would like to first hear what the Medical Officer has to say regarding this matter in general, sir."

"Very well, Captain Warren please proceed."

A smallish grey haired man shuffles some papers. He fixes his round wire-rimmed glasses, which make him look like an Owl, and begins. "It is the opinion of the medical wing of the Canadian Armed Forces that, even though homosexual activity is now legal in Canada, we still consider it a mental illness. It has been our observations that homosexual persons suffer from a wide-range of anti-social behaviour such as illicit drug use and alcoholism. Lieutenant Whitelaw."

"Yes, sir?"

"Have you ever indulged in illegal drugs such as smoking marijuana?"

Jim hesitates, and then says, "I have occasionally, sir."

"How occasionally might that be Lieutenant?"

"Perhaps a couple of times per month, sir."

"Mmmhmm."

"How would you rate your consumption of alcohol? Occasionally? Social drinker? Or do you find you need at least a couple of drinks every evening?"

189

"Social drinker, sir."

"I see. Lieutenant Menzies, have you ever indulged in illegal drugs such as smoking marijuana?"

"No, sir."

"How would you rate your consumption of alcohol? Occasionally? Social drinker? Or do you find you need at least a couple of drinks every evening?"

"Social drinker, sir."

Captain Warren looks at the other members of the tribunal and says, "That's all I have to say for now."

"Captain Whelan," says Major Winfield, "You may proceed."

"The following," he begins, "is a statement of offence as indicated under the National Defence Act Section 92 paragraph 2, that Lieutenant James Michael Whitelaw did behave in a scandalous manner unbecoming an officer. In that he, on several occasions, did knowingly and willingly commit homosexual acts with unknown males while being photographed. To add to this, he did commit these acts while wearing articles of his Canadian Armed Forces uniform."

He rests the papers he's holding on the table.

"When Major Winfield contacted me to look into the matter of Lieutenant Whitelaw's homosexual activity, I knew that in order for the S.I.U. to get the information needed; we would have to recruit someone who would be willing, not only to win Lieutenant Whitelaw's trust, but infiltrate the local homosexual scene. Captain Tyler Braid was willing to do just that, and spent the months of January to April of this year investigating Lieutenant Whitelaw's every move. Under the guise of being interested in having a homosexual relationship with Lieutenant Whitelaw, he infiltrated his circle of friends, and went to many of the places where homosexuals frequent."

Jim is squirming in his chair.

"Captain Braid recently filed a report to both the Special Investigations Unit and to members of this tribunal. This brings us to the reason for Lieutenant Menzies' presence here. For the record, Lieutenant Menzies are you homosexual?"

"I... yes, sir."

"Have you been to places where homosexuals are known to gather?"

"Yes, sir."

"Do you have friends who are homosexual?"

"Yes, sir."

"Are any of those friends in the military?"

"All civilian, sir."

"According to this report, Lieutenant Menzies, you, Lieutenant Whitelaw and a civilian male have been involved in a three-way homosexual affair for several months, is this true?"

"We were, sir."

"You were. But you're not now?"

"No, sir." Out of my peripheral vision I can see Jim's head quickly turn toward me. I continue looking straight ahead. Captain Whelan goes back to his place at the table, takes the stack of papers once more and begins to read.

"Acting upon information gathered in Captain Braid's report, the Special Investigations Unit did obtain a search warrant under Section 92, Article 106.04 of the National Defence Act. Captain Braid reported that Lieutenant Whitelaw showed him the photos which now appear before you, and Captain Braid was able to direct us to the exact location of these photos in Lieutenant Whitelaw's quarters."

He brings a small stack of Polaroids back to us and puts it in front of Jim. "Lieutenant Whitelaw, do these photos belong to you?" Jim looks through them and says, "Yes."

"How about these photos Lieutenant?" Captain Whelan places another small stack of Polaroids in front of Jim "Do these belong to you?"

I can see as Jim sorts through them, they are photos of him being tied up while wearing parts of his uniform and being penetrated by guys wearing black leather.

"Yes, sir," Jim says in a meek voice.

"I didn't hear you, Lieutenant."

"Yes, sir!"

"Let the records show that Lieutenant Whitelaw has admitted these photos belong to him. You seem to enjoy sadomasochistic sex, don't you, Lieutenant?"

"Yes, sir," Jim's voice quavers.

"You like being tied up and whipped don't you?"

"Yes, sir."

"We also see that you like to have your picture taken while you're having sex. You do enjoy that don't you?"

"Yes, sir."

"Medical Officer Warren in your professional opinion, are Lieutenant Whitelaw's sadomasochistic tendencies something we should be concerned about?"

Captain Warren clears his throat and says, "Yes. It is my professional opinion, given the evidence put before me, Lieutenant Whitelaw seems to have displayed anti-social behaviour which should be of concern to other officers."

"Could you explain, Captain?" asks Major Winfield.

"My concern lies on three fronts: one, Lieutenant Whitelaw's flagrant disrespect for the uniform of Her Majesty's Canadian Armed Forces. How can he be expected to carry out his duties in a respectful and dutiful manner when he has clearly worn articles of his uniform while engaging in sadomasochistic homosexual acts, all this while being photographed by, we assume, unknown males no less. My second concern is Lieutenant Whitelaw's indulgence in sadomasochistic activity in the first place. I am concerned about how this will affect his judgment with the men who would be placed under his command. Will they become the subjects of his sadomasochistic desires? This leads me to my third concern, how will this, in fact, affect the morale of the men placed in his command? Will they be afraid of becoming the object of his desires? As you can see this brings up a lot of important questions and concerns as far as the Medical Wing of the Armed Forces is concerned."

"Thank you, Captain Warren," says Major Winfield. "You may continue, Captain Whelan."

"It is the opinion of The Special Investigations Unit that Lieutenant James Whitelaw had a duty to be an example to, not only any men under his command, but to the general public. As an officer in Her Majesty's Canadian Armed Services it is his duty to uphold the reputation of a uniformed officer. In behaving in the reckless and scandalous manner he has, Lieutenant Whitelaw has demonstrated that not only is he a security threat, but he has a total lack of respect for the uniform of the Canadian Armed Forces. As well, he has demonstrated a lack of respect for his position as an officer in the forces. In short, he has demonstrated to all of us that he is unfit for duty. It is the recommendation of the Special Investigations Unit that Lieutenant Whitelaw be stripped of his position and dismissed from the Armed Services under Section 92 of the National Defence Act."

Captain Whelan takes his seat at the head table once more. The hush in the room roars.

"Lieutenant Whitelaw," says Major Winfield, "the evidence before this tribunal is irrefutable. Do you have anything to say?"

Jim draws a deep breath and with a quaver still in his voice says, "Major Winfield, all I can say is I know the things that I have done. I regret I've been an embarrassment to Her Majesty's Canadian Armed Forces, and I'm prepared to take the consequences of my actions. I deny making any sexual advances to either Lieutenants Harrington or Sloan. I do not know their reasons for making those accusations, but that is not important anymore. My biggest regret is that my actions have caused Lieutenant Menzies to be brought before you. I don't think he's deserved this, sir. And that's all I have to say."

"Very well, Lieutenant," says Major Winfield, "please rise."

Jim stands.

"Section 92 of the National Defence Act states, 'Every officer who behaves in a scandalous manner unbecoming an officer is guilty of an offence and on conviction shall suffer dismissal with disgrace from Her Majesty's service, or dismissal from Her Majesty's service.' Lieutenant James Michael Whitelaw these charges against you stand. You are hereby released immediately from duty. Armed guards will escort you to your quarters. You are to remove your personal belongings, and everything of an official nature will be turned over to the guards on watch. Let the record show that you will never be awarded the privilege of serving in Her Majesty's Canadian Armed Forces as long as you shall live. Is that understood?"

"Yes, sir."

"Guards, escort this man to his quarters and set up an armed post to be kept outside of his room until he removes his personal belongings. He will turn all articles of an official nature over to you. When he has packed his things, you will escort him to the main gate of the base, and you will not leave your posts until you ensure that he is well off the base. Take him away."

The two guards behind us snap to attention and march to either side of Jim.

"About turn!" yells one of the guards.

The three of them turn toward the double doors of the room.

The one guard gives the command, and the three of them leave the room.

I close my eyes once more as the sound of the metal cleats hitting the cement floor in military rhythm disappears out the door then fades. The sound of the outside door of the building slamming shut once again echoes through the hall. Then silence. Cadaver-like silence. It feels like Jim has just been executed.

"Lieutenant Bryn Thomas Menzies, please rise."

I slowly do so, and as I do I can almost feel a noose being slipped around my neck.

"The tribunal has in its possession a letter written on your behalf by your Commanding Officer. It is Captain Butler's position that you are a model officer, and have a great future ahead of you in the Forces. He describes you as respectful, well liked, and exemplary in carrying out your duties. We have seriously considered this letter, and as a result we have had a look at your record. We agree with Captain Butler's assessments. However the fact that you have had a homosexual affair with James Whitelaw gives us cause for concern. There is no way we can risk the two of you having contact ever again. Therefore, in three weeks time you will report to your new commanding officer at the Base in Halifax Nova Scotia. Captain Butler will provide details to you tomorrow morning, is that understood?"

"Yes, sir."

"You are hereby dismissed."

∞

I look around this empty apartment that I used to call mine. The laughter and the tenderness that the three of us shared for these months echo in my ears like ghosts. Halifax seems so far away, and in many ways I'll miss Calgary. But in going through the tribunal and all of this hassle with Jim, I'm also glad to be leaving. I haven't seen Jim since the tribunal. I guess he took me at my word that I didn't want to see him again.

My reminiscing is interrupted by the sound of the apartment door opening. Marcel enters the room, "Are you ready to go?"

"Yeah, I guess I am."

"I was over at David's place. I took the last of Jim's stuff over to him."

"Was Jim there?"

"Yeah."

"How is he doing?"

"He says he's okay, but he looks really sad. Do you still blame him for what happened?"

"I don't know, Marcel. I don't know anything anymore."

"He says he still loves us."

I don't know what to say or do other than look at the sad brown rug on the floor. I put my arms around Marcel and hold him close to me. "How did things come to this? When did things start spiralling out of control, Marcel?"

He puts his head on my chest. "I don't know, Bryn," he says in that wonderful Acadian accent. "But one thing I do know, we'll be starting a new life together in Halifax."

I smile and kiss him. "I'm so glad you've decided to come with me, Marcel."

"Well Bryn, Calgary's nice, but it isn't home. In Halifax I'll be close to my family in New Brunswick. And besides, I'll be with you too. I've wanted to be with you since that night I first saw you almost a year ago."

"That's right, it was almost a year ago that we met."

"You had just arrived in Calgary that afternoon."

I feel my smile grow as it all comes back to me, "Yeah, it was my first time in any sort of gay organization."

"And look at you now," Marcel smiles, "you've gone from an uptight, anal-retentive military officer, to an out gay kinkoid."

Laughter leaps out of my belly and ricochets off the empty walls. Then I hold him close and kiss him.

"Well if we're going to arrive in Halifax," Marcel says, "we should be leaving Calgary."

"You're right as usual."

"I'll remember you said that"

"I'm sure you won't let me forget."

"You kiss my be-harse."

I laugh, and pick up the small bag that I didn't pack away. We exit the apartment, and I lock the door. We go down to the main floor where the landlord lives, turn in our keys and say our goodbyes.

We walk out to the parking lot and get into the car. I start the engine, and we drive through downtown and turn eastward. Just before we reach the city limits, I turn to Marcel and say, "I want to make one last pit stop before we leave this city." Marcel nods his head as we turn into a parking lot.

"This is the first place I stopped at when I came to Calgary. I just want to check it out one last time before we leave," I say. Marcel smiles and follows me inside.

We enter the truck stop and country music still plays from the jukebox. There she is, still behind the cash register greeting people as they come in, the lady with the candy floss hair who looks like a plucked chicken.

"May I help you gentlemen," she smiles,

"Where's your washroom?" Marcel pipes up.

"Just down this hall to my left, sir," she says indicating a small hallway to her side.

Marcel disappears down the hall saying, "I'll be right back."

"I'll just wait for him," I say to the plucked chicken.

She smiles and goes back to what she was doing. I pick up a copy of the Calgary Sun and feign interest in it while I look around the dining area.

The half naked road workers that were outside about a year ago, have moved on. And the chaos of construction is now a thorough-fare clogged with late-morning traffic. There's the booth by the far window where I sat contemplating what happened between Neil and me. I vowed my life would be different, and I got what I asked for.

"You ready?" Marcel's voice startles me.

"That was fast," I say.

I put the newspaper back on the rack; we go back out to the parking lot, and Marcel gets into the car. I open the driver's door but the Calgary skyline catches my attention one last time. I feel a little emotion rise in my throat.

"Goodbye, Jim," I quietly say and get into the car.

"Are you okay?" Marcel says, rubbing my leg up and down.

"Marcel, I'm fine, and we'll be fine."

"Well, what are we waiting for?"

"Yeah, what are we waiting for?"

I start the car, and turn up the radio as Kenny Loggins sings *This Is it,* and we turn onto the Trans-Canada Highway for Nova Scotia.

To be continued...

MANY THANKS TO:

My life partner Steven Foster for all of your love and understanding and for putting up with my many whims and shenanigans over the years.

The front cover photo was taken by me in 1979. A big Thank You to Clark Nikolai for taking the back cover photo of me, January 2013.

To Jessie, David, and my family for supporting my creative efforts.

Tony Costantino and Kelly Mahoney for over half a lifetime and two provinces worth of a fantastic, ever-growing friendship!

A warm call out to Dr. Stuart Sanders of Calgary.

A big hug to Linda Nyeste also of Calgary, you and I go back to our teenage years, Love Ya!

Thanks to Karen X. Tulchinsky - for your editing skills and ongoing advice, and to James C. Johnstone - for same, and introducing me to a really great author, Jay B. Laws.

The Members of the Monthly Writing Group: Georgina Daniels, Sheila Smart, Dr. Pega Ren, Stephen Emery, Brian Frazier, Claude Hewitt, Eric Brown, Bennet, Tyler Tone, Ken Tomilson, Steven Kates, and Gerry McCadden for your suggestions and for being there.

My Peer Editors: Steven Foster, Ed Stringer, Gerald Goldie, Don Durrell of Vancouver and Richard Beamish of Budapest, Hungary for your willingness to assist.

To Stephen Locke of Speak Sebastian Radio in Calgary, for supplying me with long-forgotten information about the Calgary gay community from the late seventies/early eighties; and thanks also to Dr. Bruce Freeman also of Calgary for your advice.

To all of the GLBT Community who lived through the "in-between" years, 1979 to 1983, (the end of the heyday of gay liberation, and the arrival of the first major wave of AIDS). To the warriors we've lost, and to better times ahead. And to all of those wonderful people, too numerous to mention here, who have supported my creative efforts along the way.

The information for the Military Tribunal scene in Bryn's story came from:

The Queen's Regulations and Orders for the Canadian Army, Volume 2 (Disciplinary)

(As amended up to and including Amendment List 81 dated 1 March 1965)

Issued under the authority of the National Defence Act

Art. 103.25–SCANDALOUS CONDUCT BY OFFICERS

Section 83 of *The National Defence Act* provides:

"83. Every Officer who behaves in a scandalous manner unbecoming an officer is guilty of an offence and on conviction shall suffer dismissal with disgrace from Her Majesty's service or dismissal from Her Majesty's service."

The statement of the offence in a charge under section 83 should be in the following form:

Behaved in a scandalous manner unbecoming an officer

CPSIA information can be obtained at www.ICGtesting.com
Printed in the USA
LVOW08s0730170813

348297LV00001B/12/P